LEGENDS OF
SPIRIT WOODS

Campfire tales from Northern Wisconsin by

Craig Hackett

www.ten16press.com - Waukesha, WI

Legends of Spirit Woods
Copyrighted © 2016, 2021 Craig Hackett
Second Edition

Legends of Spirit Woods
by Craig Hackett
ISBN 978-1-943331-19-2

For information, please contact:

www.ten16press.com
Waukesha, WI

Cover photo © Holly Belsey

With the sole exception of "Christmas 1942" which is based on a true event that happened to the author's father, all stories included in this book are fiction and the product of the authors imagination. Any similarities to actual events are strictly coincidental and it's probably borderline miraculous if they are similar.

To Pauline Helt-Hackett:
A mother who refused to give up on her youngest son.
Thanks Mom.

For
My Boys: Mark, Danny & Bryan

My Nieces: Christine, Dana, Nina & Ann Clara

My Nephew: Benjamin

Table of Contents

The Grisly Fate of Johnny Rotten

Once there was a young couple that was looking to buy some property in Vilas County, Wisconsin. The realtor they were working with had found a potential home on Eagle Lake and wanted to meet with the couple there to show them. It was early evening when the young couple, following the realtor's instructions, turned onto Eagle Lake Road. They were chatting excitedly about their potential purchase when suddenly, in the middle of the road, seemingly from nowhere, appeared a horrendous sight. The husband slammed on the brakes, and he and his wife watched in disbelief as a man, clothes on fire, staggered slowly towards them in an agonizing shuffle. Just before he reached the front of their car he collapsed. The man and his wife got out of their car and ran to the front. To their disbelief they found . . . nothing.

I'm certain everyone has heard the stories of gangland Chicago during the 1920s, where making money through any means possible, legal or illegal, was the doctrine and violence was as common as pigeons on a statue. Any communication between the different groups of mobsters trying to gain control of the Chicago underworld was usually delivered by the business end of a Thompson submachine gun. Many a bullet-riddled corpse that turned up in the alleys or the Chicago River testified to this fact.

It is well documented how these men who pursued their fortunes in less than ethical ways would often hide out in northern Wisconsin when the "heat" of the local authorities became too intense for their liking, but sometimes the violence that these villains tried to escape would find them even in the solitude of the North Woods.

In this dark underworld there was never a lack of people willing to carry out the orders of a mob boss. Men with morals or conscience were not found among them; neither were the faint of heart. Amidst these evil guns for hire was a man named John Rattan, or "Johnny Rotten," as he was called. A former church altar boy, he had turned from his religious upbringing and was now a favorite of the undisputed crime boss of Chicago, Al Capone. Johnny had made a name for himself at a young age as a cold-blooded killer. Most hired guns did not care to murder people but would shrug it off as part of the job and try and think about the money they made carrying out the bidding of the mob boss. They also knew that failure to complete the job would most likely mean someone would be sent to kill them.

Johnny Rotten was not that way. He enjoyed killing and was proud of his evil reputation. Once during a drive-by "hit," he jumped out of the vehicle he was in and stood unprotected in the middle of the street and shot it out with four members of a rival gang. Eye witnesses later testified he was laughing as he meticulously gunned down the four with his machine gun. Johnny feared nothing or no one, and Capone was more than willing to pay handsomely for his services.

One particularly gruesome case involved a small-time gangster that had stolen a truck loaded with Capone's bootleg whiskey. Capone sent Johnny Rotten, who found the petty thief and dealt with him. The hood's body was found several days later early in the morning in the middle of Main Street, downtown Chicago. Johnny had purposely dragged him there behind his car and left his body in plain sight for all to see. The police autopsy report indicated that the man had been the victim of hours of inhumane torture. Capone himself commented once that Johnny had a sadistic streak in him like he had never seen before. The message to the rest of gangland Chicago, however, was clear: Capone's whiskey was off limits.

With the money Johnny made, he lived like a king during a time when most of the country was out of work and starving. Well, the years passed and Capone was eventually convicted of tax evasion even though he was guilty of dozens of other crimes more sinister and sent to prison. With Capone behind bars Johnny Rotten decided that he was going to take over the gang. He made it clear that he was not just keeping Capone's seat warm until he got back, but that it was now his gang. He didn't figure that Capone could touch him from prison.

Capone, however, as Johnny Rotten was about to find out, had a long reach, even from Eastern State Penitentiary on the far side of the country. Rotten was raking in tons of Capone's money, and all Capone could do was wait and bide his time as he sat in prison. Finally, after personally gunning down two Chicago Police officers "just for the fun of it," Johnny decided to go spend some time at Capone's hideout in Vilas County until things quieted down a bit. It was here Capone had his men set a trap. Johnny stayed at Capone's hideaway for a few days, then got bored and decided he wanted to go to the town of Eagle River for supper. After dinner, as Johnny walked down the street, a stranger asked him for a match. Johnny reached into his pocket and at the same time he was struck from behind by a man that had been waiting unseen in a dark doorway. Next thing he knew, he was tied up and shoved into the trunk of a car.

The car drove east out of town to what is today Eagle Lake Road. There Johnny was pulled from the trunk and in the glow of the car headlights was severely beaten by four or five of Capone's henchmen. Comeuppance was long overdue and Johnny was getting it all at once. Finally, the beating finished, Johnny was shot and dumped in a shallow grave on the side of the road. Logs and brush were piled on top of him, gasoline was added, and finally a match. Flames erupted, and then, much to everyone's surprise, a terrible, horrifying scream rose from the funeral pyre. Rotten was not dead and was suffering a most unspeakable torture. The gangster gunned the burning pile then jumped into the car and sped off, leaving Johnny Rotten to his well-deserved fate.

The next morning the sheriff went to investigate the thin column of smoke he had seen from town. Arriving at the scene he was shocked to find the charred remains of a man lying in the road, nearby the still smoldering grave. It was indeed Johnny Rotten. Before he died he had managed to crawl out of the burning ditch and stagger onto the road—a feat in itself because he had two broken arms and a broken leg, as well as being burnt to a crisp. The sheriff later equated it to seeing a condemned soul try and escape the fires of hell. He may have been more right than he imagined. An investigation turned up nothing, and over time the case was forgotten. Johnny's remains were returned to Chicago and buried in the churchyard of Saint Frederick's Cathedral, where he once served as an altar boy.

The story, however, does not end here. Capone reportedly went insane in prison. Screaming like a mad man night after night, claiming that the charred corpse of Johnny Rotten was in his cell. After Capone was released from prison, he went to live in Florida, where he died completely mad after years of insisting that burned and battered Johnny Rotten was always in the room with him; if he was, only Capone could see him.

After Capone's death in 1947 rumors began to circulate in the Eagle River area of an apparition that roamed between Otter Lake and Eagle Lake. Many hunters and fishermen reported encountering what appeared to be a horribly burned and disfigured man that would appear from nowhere, say nothing and disappearing after only a few moments. Others claimed hearing a terrifying scream coming from thin air only feet away from them.

There was a man that bought some property on the south shore of Otter Lake near the spot Rotten met his demise. He scoffed at the ghost stories—"pure nonsense," he called them. He then camped on his land for several weeks in fall and built himself a dock for his boat. He went out fishing and was only a few yards from shore when he turned back to look at his property. There standing on his newly built dock was a shocking sight. A man blackened by fire, his arms hanging limp at his side, stared out at him with hollow eyes. It was such a horror, he had to turn away. When he looked back, the man was gone. That night, still shaken by what he had seen, the man nervously built a large fire and just as he began to cook the fish he had caught, he was mortified by a horrible scream like that of a banshee coming from the fire itself. This was too much for the man. He left Otter Lake that night, later sold the property, and never returned to Vilas County. He apparently had supplies delivered to build a home including a bath tub, which to this day remains where he left it, half buried by years of neglect.

The land passed through a dozen owners over the next several decades. All who owned the property claimed to have encountered the terrible ghost of Johnny Rotten. One owner hired a psychic, who held a séance near the spot of the murder and claimed to learn that Johnny Rotten, due to wrongs he had committed, was condemned to wander the Earth without rest, continuously reliving the last moments of his mortal life. His broken bones cause him incredible agony, but the thing that tortures him the most is when someone lights a fire in the proximity of the spot he died; he relives the horrible torment of flames searing his flesh. His spirit has been seen regularly in the area he died. But it is most commonly encountered in fall around the time he breathed his last earthly breath.

The Ghost of the Widow's Walk

The waning years of the nineteenth century on the Great Lakes saw the dawn of the steel freighter era. The predecessors of today's super tankers were born into a time that still saw a large majority of commerce carried out by wooden ships. During this transition, it was not long before heavy steel bows met wooden hulls, often with devastating results. One such incident occurred near Isle Royale in Lake Superior. The wooden lumber schooner *St. George*, while carrying James Dudeck's Wild Animal Show, was run down in heavy fog by a steel-hulled vessel. The *St. George* and all who sailed on her that fateful night were lost to the frigid depth of Lake Superior.

The master of the *St. George* was Captain Tom Lander. Captain Lander had sailed the Great Lakes for forty-plus years, and this was to be his final trip before turning command of the *St. George* over to his first officer and retiring to his home on a bluff overlooking the lake at Marquette, Michigan. Unfortunately, Captain Lander never saw his home again.

For years after Lander's death, ships coming into Marquette Harbor could clearly see Margie Lander, the captain's widow, pacing the upper porch of her house overlooking the harbor. Always dressed in a black cloak, she spent her days watching the horizon for the return of her beloved husband. In a strange way she became a ray of hope for weary sailors, especially at night when she walked the upper porch of her house with a lantern that more than once helped guide lost ships safely into the harbor. Ships leaving or returning to Marquette Harbor would ring their bell in respect to Margie and her long-lost husband.

Once in late November, which as seasoned sailors know is a dangerous time to be on the lake, a small schooner was returning to Marquette Harbor after being out for more than three months. Still miles from her destination, the ship was caught in a terrific storm on the open lake and was pounded mercilessly with wind and freezing rain. Visibility fell to almost zero, and soon the small schooner began to break apart. Several sailors were washed overboard into eternity, their cries for help lost in the howling wind.

Suddenly, Nathan, the first mate, spotted something through the torrent of wind and rain. "Margie's light!!" he shouted as he pointed into the wicked torrent. The helmsman immediately steered for faint glow in the distance. The small schooner, badly leaking and barely afloat, reached the harbor entrance just as a monstrous wave smashed down upon her. All remaining crew members where thrown into the wild tempest as the ship quickly capsized and sank, erased as if she never existed. Even though the harbor offered some shelter from the storm, the waves were still considerable, and the near-freezing water quickly doomed the remainder of the crew. Soon all that remained was Nathan, the first mate. He struggled desperately through the waves, fighting his way towards the only thing he could see, the light of Margie's lantern. Yards from shore, he finally ran out strength. Inches from salvation, he could fight no more. Just before he slipped beneath the waves, Nathan saw a figure shrouded in a black cloak wade into the water and felt a hand grab him by the collar and drag him up on the sand. Next thing he knew he was being carried down the beach by the surfboat crew of the Marquette lifesaving station. They took Nathan to the station, where he quickly regained consciousness.

"Who pulled me out?" Nathan asked, wishing to thank the person.

All the lifesavers shrugged. "We found you on the beach," replied one.

"We saw the glow of your lamp, and when we went to investigate, there you were out cold, your lantern glowing by your noggin."

Nathan shrugged. "I didn't have a lantern; it must be Margie Lander's. We saw her light when were still out on the lake. She must have seen I was in trouble and ran down to the beach to help me."

The surfboat men all glanced at each other. Finally the captain of the rescue crew cleared his throat and spoke. "Margie Lander died more than two months ago. Her daughter went to visit her and found her on the ground outside of her home. Doc said she had a stroke and fell from the widow's walk; she was dead when her daughter found her. They buried her on the bluff near her home so she could watch the boats come and go."

A chill went down Nathan's spine. He shuddered then said, "It must be somebody else, then."

The surfboat captain shook his head. "There ain't no one else around here. The next house isn't for five miles, and no one is out on a night like this."

The next morning, the weather having cleared, Nathan took the old lantern and walked up the bluff to Margie's old house. Now vacant with the windows boarded up, it was apparent that no one had been there in weeks. Nathan placed the lantern on the front step, whispered, "Thank you," and left. For years afterwards many sailors who had been lost on the lake claimed they were guided home by a light high on the bluff from the former home of Margie Lander. These claims did not cease until decades later when a light house was built marking the entrance of the harbor. Some say the lighthouse allowed Margie to find peace and allowed her to finally rest. Years later, the Lander house, now in disrepair, burned to the ground. Today a field of wild flowers covers the area where the house once stood. Margie's grave remains nearby on the bluff overlooking the harbor, though it is rarely visited. As for Nathan, he never returned to sail the Great Lakes. He took his wife, Molly, and they moved to Eagle River, but that's a story for another time.

The Horror at Hobo Spring

I am certain most of you know the history of Waukesha County and how it gained fame in the late nineteenth and early twentieth centuries when people from all over the world flocked there to drink water from numerous fresh-water springs that promised to cure whatever was ailing you. With names like Hygeia, Bethesda, Still Rock, Acme and Minneska, there were plenty of choices for those seeking to drink the life-giving water.

Today most of the springs are gone, covered over, buried or forgotten all together. Only a few remain, and the number of people that actually remember the springs in their heyday is rapidly diminishing.

It had been a long, frustrating day at work, you know the kind—your boss is a jerk and the stupidest man on earth and he is picking on you for nonsense and spouting, "Do I have to do everything around here?" and it feels like the whole world is against you. As if this wasn't enough, when my shift ended I found my car decided to gang up on me too and refused to start. Wallowing in self-pity, I decided to walk home. Abandoning my car only after giving the tire a good swift kick and pronouncing it a stupid pile of junk, I began my five-mile trek towards home. Since it was only slightly out of my way and thinking it would calm my already frazzled nerves, I opted to utilize the paved walkway along the Fox River. It was here while walking through Frame Park that I stopped by Hobo Spring.

Now as far as the popularity of Waukesha springs, Hobo is way down the list. Unlike Bethesda or Hygeia, whose water was bottled and shipped worldwide, Hobo Spring was frequented by those that chose to live largely in society's shadows. Some were fugitives from the law, others down on their luck and running from their past, still others were driven by drug or alcohol problems. These types were known largely as "hobos," generally people who were harmless but you were probably better off to avoid them.

The location of Hobo Spring near the Minneapolis, St. Paul and Sault Ste. Marie (also known as the "Soo Line") rail yards in Waukesha made it a prime spot for weary bums to take a break and drink from the cool water. When I was a kid the father of a friend of mine worked for the railroad and told us never to go to Hobo Spring after dark, that it was "haunted." At first that frightened me but as I grew older I figured it was just my friend's father trying to give us a scare and maybe indirectly telling us not to play around the nearby tracks. Whatever it was, ghosts were not my concern when I decided to take a break from my walk.

I sat down by the little bubbling pool and must have been more tired than I realized because I think I fell asleep. The next thing I knew the sun had set, and to my shock there were five or six hobos sitting around the spring with me. Startled, I began to get up when something pushed me back down with considerable force and held me there. I say "something" because the pressure on my shoulder did not feel like a human hand. It felt callous and claw-like, and I could not escape its grasp. I tried struggling but the grip was far too great, and whatever it was then hissed in my ear, "*Shadowsssss*," drawing out the "S" sound. "*They can't seeeee yoooou.*"

Frightened, my mind racing off in several directions at once, I managed to choke out, "What do you want?"

The hissing voice replied, "*Waatch.*" As I looked upon the scene before my eyes, I saw the hobos taking turns drinking from the spring. After they all had their fill they sat back to relax. Suddenly one of them doubled over in pain and began to make the groaning sounds of a man dying in pain. Before the others could render him any help, another of the men collapsed, then another; soon all of the men were writhing in some tortured agony, all foaming at the mouth as if some horrendous creature were about to burst out of them.

Terrified as I watched the horrible sight before me, I managed to ask, "What is wrong with them?"

This time the answer came in the form of what I think was a disembodied arm with a boney claw where the hand should have been. It managed to point at the little spring and I heard *"Poison"* hissed into my ear.

"Who poisoned it?" I asked breathlessly. This time there was no answer, only what seemed an eternity as I was forced to watch the men succumb to the poison one by one until they all lay so still I knew they were dead.

When the last one stopped moving, like a stage play two other men came into view, standing almost right in front of me. One was dressed as a security guard with a round patch on his chest saying "Soo Line Railway." The other man was wearing a gray suit and blue tie. It was clear by his upright posture and unwavering gaze into the security guard's eyes that the well-dressed man was the boss of the rail yard.

"I told you to get rid of those bums," he screamed at the guard.

The guard replied, "They're just trying to get a drink of water. They're not hurting anything."

Still shouting, the boss replied, "Do I have to do everything around here? FINE! I'll take care of it! You're fired!"

As those two faded from view I came to believe that the creature holding me there and making me watch was some demonic spirit of yard boss himself. "You killed them," I said, gaining a little boldness in my voice.

"Noooo!" I heard. Sitting there unable to move, I could now see the depths of the murderer's crime as images of him dragging the bodies one by one to the nearby Fox River, throwing them

in and walking away without a single shred of remorse, faded in and out of view in front of my eyes, like an UHF channel on an old black and white television set. I could see his other crimes as well—stealing, cheating, bullying—but all paled in comparison to the murder of the men at the spring.

Then without warning an image came into sharp focus. There before me was the spirit of the yard boss, bound for who knows how long to Hobo Spring with a burning thirst. He was still wearing the remains of his gray suit, except now it was threadbare and hung off his bony frame like a wrinkled suit on a wire hanger. He knelt before the spring and tried to drink but when he leaned over, the water would retreat, always staying inches from his mouth. I then saw him use his hands to try and scoop the water but the few pitiful drops he managed to capture dried and turned to ash before he could drink. He then looked right at me and extended his upturned hands pleading for help. I sat horrified until this image too faded from view. It was then I was released from the demon's grasp. But before I could run away I clearly heard one last thing that shook me to my core: *"Room for one more."*

I ran for home and never once looked back. The entire episode is burned forever into my memory and there is a mark on my shoulder where the demon's claw held me down. I can still see the images of the shadows at the spring and their tortured agony. But the one thing that sticks in my mind as I reflect upon what I think I saw is the idea that maybe my day hadn't been so bad after all.

The Revenge of Corporal Ray

1700 hours, mail call.

"SERGEANT VANDERGRAFF."
"HERE."

In a scene that has been repeated since the dawn of the warfare, a group of soldiers gathered around a single officer distributing mail. The only thing different this time was the location, Mosul, Iraq.

Sergeant Steven Vandergraff, or "Van" as his friends called him, was from St. Germain, Wisconsin. Van originally enlisted in the US Army in 1990 and had fought in Desert Storm, for which he received a Medal of Valor as a result of a skirmish with the Iraqi Republican Guard in the Kuwaiti desert. When that war was over, he served in Somalia. After eight years of distinguished service both in the US and overseas, he left the Army and returned home to Vilas County. He got a job working for the county and spent his free time fishing the local rivers and lakes. He also joined a Civil War reenactment group where he regularly portrayed Corporal Joshua Ray, a Union Cavalry soldier from Major John Crandall's 1st Cavalry unit.

Both Major Crandall and Corporal Ray were from upper Wisconsin, Crandall from Rhinelander and Ray from St. Germain. Both men had served with distinction. Ray enlisted in the US Cavalry in 1862 when he was just eighteen years old, and after two years of fighting, was killed in the Shenandoah Valley in 1864.

Major Crandall survived the Civil War and spent the rest of his life in Vilas County living in virtual anonymity.

About a year after the beginning of the invasion of Iraq, Van, who had been home for just under two years, was recalled by the Army and sent to the conflict. His assigned tour was eighteen months, and he was nearing the end of this stretch. Van had seen his share of firefights and ambushes, had lost a few friends and inflicted numerous casualties against insurgents. Tomorrow was scheduled to be his last patrol before he began his rotation home, and he was both nervous and excited—excited at the prospect that he would soon be going home, and nervous because the last two sergeants from his unit to be killed had been killed on their last patrols.

The fact that he had received mail today helped lighten his mood. He returned to his bunker and using his K-bar knife opened a letter from his dad. Inside was the usual stuff a father would write to his son: weather, local gossip and fishing-related stories. Also included was a photograph taken during the last Civil War reenactment encampment he had attended before being recalled. Van smiled as he remembered the good time he had had at the encampment and looked forward to getting back home.

A moment later a runner stuck his head in Van's bunker. "Briefing at the O-P now," he said.

Van grabbed his rifle and headed for the operations post. Once inside, the commanding officer rolled out a map and outlined the plan for tomorrow's patrol. They were to investigate several homes that had been cleared previously of insurgents and thought to be safe. The briefing was to the point. He outlined the plan and a route that would take them to a part of the city they had very little intelligence about but was not suspected to be a terrorist stronghold. The CO concluded with, "We will be sending along a member of the local militia to act as guide and interpreter. He assures me the area is safe. This is not expected to get ugly."

Van returned to his bunker and lay down for the night; he reread his dad's letter and fell asleep staring at the picture his dad had sent. Falling into a deep sleep he dreamed he was back home attending one of the Civil War reenactment encampments. In his dream he was sitting alone by a campfire. Across from him he heard someone begin playing a harmonica. In the low light he couldn't see who it was so Van placed a couple of more logs on the fire, and in a few minutes when the fire grew he could make out the dim outline of ragged-looking Cavalry soldier across the fire pit playing a melancholy tune.

"Strange," Van thought to himself. He hadn't recalled seeing this man before. The stranger played for a few more minutes, and then abruptly he wiped off his harmonica and put it in his pocket.

"Gonna be a rough one tomorrow, Van," he said. Van nodded his head. "Watch out for treachery tomorrow," the stranger added.

Before Van could ask what that meant, the fire popped and flared for a moment, blinding him. When the fire went down, the Cavalry soldier was gone. Van woke with a start. The dream had seemed so real it took him a moment to realize he wasn't back home, but in a place far removed.

At that same instant the commanding officer's runner came in to wake him. "It's time," he said.

Van gathered his equipment, checked his rifle and joined his squad at the motor pool. They took two Humvees, and under the direction of the Iraqi militia guide, they were soon on their way to a far corner of Mosul. Arriving at the location, the soldiers exited the hummers and took up defense positions as part of the standard operating procedures. It was very quiet. Too quiet, Van thought to himself, like the entire neighborhood was abandoned; no kids playing, no animals, and no activity of any kind.

Suddenly Van heard a harmonica playing the same melancholy tune he had heard in his dream the night before. He turned and the saw their Iraqi guide slowly lowering his rifle at the back of one of the other American soldiers. Before he could shout a warning, a rocket-propelled grenade exploded in front of the Humvees. Simultaneously, a hail of enemy machine gunfire erupted from one of the houses they were parked in front of. Van fired blindly at the Iraqi militia guide as he shouted for his men to take cover. He dove inside the Humvee and grabbed the radio to request assistance, but before he could say a word, someone grabbed him, pulled him back out, hustled him off several yards and threw him into a ditch on the side of the road. At that very moment the vehicle was hit by an RPG, which exploded with devastating force, destroying it. The second Humvee was disabled moments later.

Van and his men were pinned down behind the burning hummers. The air was full of smoke and flying metal, they had no support, no help was coming to their aid, and the situation was beyond desperate. Van knew he had to do something. He managed to raise his head to try and locate the enemy but he could see nothing though the ever-thickening pall of smoke, flame and flying debris. The rest of the soldiers watched as Van ducked back down. They saw him grab his bayonet and fix it to his rifle. Through the use of hand gestures he ordered his men to do the same and to get ready to attack.

Next, Van grabbed a grenade, pulled the pin and threw it over the wreckage towards the nearest house. It exploded; a second later he led the men on a charge across the open area between the wrecked hummers and into the home. The soldiers, with Van in the lead, burst through the front door and raked the room with gunfire. In a matter of moments the battle was over, the insurgents defeated. Not a single member of Van's squad was seriously injured. As the smoke started to clear, one of his men found a working radio in the wreckage of the hummers. A message was sent to the base and assistance soon arrived. Van's squad stayed on the scene until it was completely secured. He and his men then hitched a ride back to the base, where they were debriefed.

A few days later Van was packed and ready to head back to the United States and eventually home to St. Germain. The CO's runner came into his bunker. "Van, the CO wants to see you."

Van followed the runner back to the CO's office, not sure what to expect. Much to his surprise the rest of his squad was waiting for him there. His squad stood at attention as the CO sat behind his desk and read a commendation letter, then presented Van with his second Medal of Valor for extreme bravery for the recent incident in Mosul.

Almost a month later, Van, now discharged from the Army, was back home in St. Germain. It was Memorial Day. Van got dressed in his Army uniform and headed to the cemetery. It was early in the morning when he arrived. It was quiet and the only person in sight was an elderly caretaker raking up a small pile of debris. Van walked up to him. "Excuse me," Van said.

The caretaker looked up from his raking and said, "Sergeant Steven Vandergraff?" Van was surprised.

"Yes," he said. "How did you know?"

"We've been expecting you," he said with the slightest hint of a smile on his face.

"We?" Van replied.

The old caretaker nodded. "Come with me," he said. "I know who you are here to see."

Van followed the man through the cemetery and listened as he explained. "I read about your incident in Iraq in the newspaper and how you were awarded the Medal of Valor for your actions. I knew then you would be coming to see Corporal Ray."

He stopped and motioned at an old white headstone. "Joshua Ray, 1st US Cavalry, Killed Shenandoah Valley 1864," Van read out loud.

It was then Van noticed something else. On a velvet cloth on the grave rested dozens of military medals. Commendations from the Spanish-American War, World War I, World War II,

Korea, Vietnam, up to and including Desert Storm. Van struggled to say something, but before he could the old caretaker started to speak. "Every medal you see here was left by a veteran who claims Corporal Ray came and helped him in a desperate situation. They say the one from the Spanish-American War is from Teddy Roosevelt himself. I cannot confirm this."

It was then Van related his story about his dream at the campfire. How the next day he thought he heard the sounds of the harmonica again and turned in time to see the Iraqi militia soldier about to open fire on him and his men. How a man wearing what appeared to be a blue Cavalry uniform pulled him out of the Humvee seconds before it was blown into oblivion. And how when he looked over the top of the burning wreckage he saw something amazing. "I didn't know where the enemy fire was coming from," Van explained. "The insurgents had us sighted in and they threw several smoke grenades to confuse us. Their plan was working well. I thought for sure we were all dead men. I knew I had to try and get a bead on where the enemy was. When I looked over the top of the hummer I couldn't see a thing through the heavy smoke and flame. Suddenly the entire world went totally silent. I couldn't hear a sound. Then I saw the same person from my dream step through the smoke with a saber in his hand. He gestured for me to follow him. I organized my men and we followed him. He led us to the enemy and we destroyed them. They assumed we were totally defenseless and they were not expecting us to attack. That soldier saved all our lives." The caretaker nodded knowingly as if he had heard the story before. Van stared at the grave in silence for a while trying to collect his thoughts.

"Ya see," the caretaker began explaining, as if sensing Van had questions, "during the Shenandoah Valley campaign the 1st Cavalry was camped along the Shenandoah River near the Virginia-West Virginia border. One night a ragged Confederate soldier came into the camp to surrender. He explained to Major

Crandall that he knew where there were several other Rebels that wanted to surrender. The next morning Crandall sent Corporal Ray and his men, which was about ten troopers, with the Confederate soldier to accept the surrender of the group of Rebel soldiers. Turns out they were led into a trap. All of the Union Cavalry were killed, gunned down before they could fire a shot in defense. Later a second patrol led by Major Crandall found Corporal Ray still barely alive. Before he died Crandall swore he would avenge him. Major Crandall kept his word. Within four weeks every single one of the Rebel soldiers that ambushed Ray and his men was either killed in fighting or captured and hung for their treachery. The last one of the group to be killed was the one that led the Union troopers into the ambush. He had eluded capture and was thought to have escaped from the Shenandoah Valley. Just when the 1st Cavalry was about to give up, the traitor was found. He had been slashed to death in an abandoned farm house. It was a gruesome sight, and the dead man had a look of utter horror frozen on what remained of his face. Lying near the Rebel's body was the saber that was used to kill him. The saber belonged to Corporal Ray. Funny thing was, when Ray's body was sent home over three weeks before, he was wearing his saber."

Van stood quietly for a moment, then said, "After I returned to the Humvees when the firefight was over, I happened to glance at the Iraqi militia soldier that had been our guide. I turned him over to see if he was dead. He was, but he wasn't shot; he had been slashed to death, and this saber was lying next to his body." Van pulled a saber from the scabbard of his dress uniform. "As you can clearly see, scratched in the handle it says, 'Joshua Ray 1st US Cavalry.' That is how I knew to come here."

Silently Van placed the saber on the Ray's grave. Next he pulled out his Medal of Valor and laid it on the velvet cloth. Then he stood at attention and saluted the grave. "Thank you, Corporal," he said.

Van turned and started to walk away, when a thought occurred to him. "How," Van asked, "did he know?"

The caretaker didn't hesitate in his response. "Before Corporal Ray died he vowed revenge against all traitors, starting with the one that betrayed him and his men. His anger towards them burns very deep, even to this day."

Van nodded and turned to give the grave one final salute. As he did he noticed the saber he placed there only moments ago was now gone. He turned at looked at the caretaker. The old man just nodded his head. "Corporal Ray clearly isn't finished yet," was all he said.

The Military Road

It was the summer after my first year in college. By all counts the preceding year had been a success: I had gotten good grades (most important, according to my dad), made some new friends, and had taken the first steps to forging myself a place in the world. It had been a bit intense, too, because from day one way back in September there had always been something to do or someplace to go. So with my first year now behind me, I suddenly had nothing to do. I did have a summer job but it was not scheduled to start for two weeks.

It was here I hit upon a bold plan. A year before I had camped near Lake Franklin in the Nicolet National Forest. While doing some exploring I discovered what appeared to be an old road, which later turned out to be what was something once called the "Military Road." This road was built during the Civil War and connected Fort Howard in Green Bay with Fort Wilkinson in the upper Keweenaw Peninsula of Michigan on the shores of Lake Superior. It was used during the Civil War to rapidly reinforce Fort Wilkinson in case of an emergency. Long before it became known as the Military Road, however, it was simply known as the "Superior Trail" and had been used for hundreds of years by Indians, trappers, copper miners and loggers. Under direct orders of Abraham Lincoln, the trail was widened and improved for wagon travel and given the name Military Road. Somehow I got the idea that it would be interesting to explore some of this nineteenth century "highway" and maybe camp out for a few nights.

Stopping at home I grabbed my small tent, some miscellaneous camping necessities, my laptop, my camera and my best friend, my dog Jet, an Australian shepherd. Borrowing my parents' Jeep, I soon was on my way to Vilas County. My plan was simple: leave the Jeep at my aunt and uncle's on Pike Lake and hike down the snowmobile trail along Highway 70 until I intercepted the Military Road.

When I stopped at Pike Lake my uncle offered me a "trap" camera to take along—you've all seen one. It is basically a waterproof box you strap to a tree near ground level. It has a sensor that will trigger the shutter of the camera when anything passes in front of it, like a person or animal. It also has a counter and a date code to show you how many pictures it has taken and the date they were taken. "You can set it up when you camp and catch photos of stuff that comes down the trail at night," he explained.

I thanked him and stuffed it into my backpack. I stayed that night on my aunt and uncle's couch and charged up the batteries for my laptop and my phone because I knew it might be several days before I was anywhere near electricity again.

Early the next morning Jet and I set off on foot down Highway 70 as planned, and after an hour or so I stopped in a small convenience store to buy some supplies. Since I didn't have a cooler, everything I bought had to be canned, so imagine my delight when I found my favorite frozen burgers in packages of two. Those would stay frozen long enough for me to cook them tonight. I piled several cans of food on the checkout counter along with my precious frozen burgers and was looking around for what else might come in handy when this old guy emerged from a room by the cash register where he had been watching TV.

He began to ring up my purchases and said, "Going to do a little camping, eh?"

"Yep," I replied, "going up to hike some of the Military Road."

"You won't like what you find there," he said. And he said it so matter-of-factly and without looking up that it took me by complete surprise.

"Why so?" I asked, getting a little defensive.

The old man shrugged. "You'll see," was all he said.

I paid for my purchase and left. Jet, who had been lying outside the door, jumped to his feet, and soon we were on our way. In about another forty-five minutes we intercepted the trail just inside of the Nicolet National Forest and began our trek northward. It wasn't the easiest path to follow due to it being overgrown and neglected the last 100 years or so, but it was not impassable. One thing I did notice almost immediately was that it was several degrees cooler in the shade of the forest than it had been out on the highway. Now, having spent more than a few days in northern Wisconsin in my lifetime, I was aware that one needed to be ready for just about any kind of weather, so it was little trouble to stop and dig out a sweatshirt. After hiking most of the day I found a good place to camp for the night.

I pitched my tent and made a small fire pit, and soon the odor of the hamburgers was drifting among the pines from my little iron skillet. It was at this point that something a bit strange occurred. I had just finished my dinner and was sitting on a rock congratulating myself on a fine meal when first I heard and then felt a cold wind snap down the trail. Jet, who was usually completely fearless, stared into the wind, snarled his meanest growl and then suddenly whimpered and ran and hid behind me. I found this troubling because it was the first time I had seen him show fear.

The year before when we were up here we encountered a bear, and without hesitation Jet chased him off. But now that same animal was cowering behind me as the wind grew to a howl and almost blew my fire out. Then, just as quickly as it had come up, it was gone. A bit unnerving but not the scariest thing I had ever seen.

After cleaning up dinner I set up the trap camera, and Jet and I went to bed. The next morning we broke camp, and as I was packing away the trap camera I saw that during the night it had taken about a dozen pictures. With no time to look I stuffed it in my backpack, and we continued north.

It was a perfect day with the sunlight filtering through the canopy of trees that had grown over the trail. We made good time and stopped for lunch in a small clearing. As we sat and ate, once again we experienced that strange sensation of the cold wind, except this time it lasted for over a minute. Again, strange but not all that terrifying, I chalked it up to an unusual atmospheric condition unique to the region and let it go at that.

After lunch we continued on and made good time for several hours. We then decided to make camp along a small creek that ran parallel to the trail just north of Highway 28 in the Upper Peninsula of Michigan. It was here we stumbled across the remains of an old logging camp. The few structures that were once there had collapsed into nearly unrecognizable piles of timber, but standing on the trail one could still make out the saw and the conveyer that had brought logs into it for cutting. I wanted to explore it, but Jet and I were hungry, so we decided to eat before investigating the camp further. I built a fire, and Jet and I shared a couple cans of ravioli. I washed the pans in the stream and, since we were in bear country, I buried the empty cans and anything else that might have attracted unwanted attention.

With that done, Jet and I explored the old logging camp. Most of the buildings had collapsed long ago, and an eerie silence hung in the air. Jet would sniff around and then every so often would perk his ears up and bark, staring intently at something I could not see. With the sun fading quickly in the east we headed back to our camp. Just before turning in I set up the trap camera on the other side of the trail and pointed it towards the tent. This would show me if anything came down the trail at night.

We didn't sleep that well, and every time I fell back to sleep I thought I could hear people talking off in the distance. Come dawn I was jolted awake by the distinct sound of a one of those big circular saws you see at sawmills, but when I got out of the tent the sound had vanished.

Pulling the trap camera off the tree, I noticed that this time it had taken several dozen pictures during the night. Wanting to get away from this creepy place, I quickly packed it up with the rest of the gear, and we headed south, back down the trail towards Franklin Lake. About noontime we stopped to have lunch. It was here I pulled out the trap camera and my laptop. I connected the camera to my computer, and in a few moments the pictures began to appear on the screen.

The first few were nothing out of the ordinary: a raccoon, a fox and a couple deer. Then the next several pictures seemed to be of nothing in particular. As a matter of fact, I couldn't see why the camera had gone off at all. Then I took a closer look and suddenly I could see what appeared to be a dim outline of a shape. I first dismissed it as a shadow but looking again I could clearly see what undeniably was a human form. And even though I could make out facial features and the clothes they were wearing I could see right through the image. Several more pictures revealed shadowy figures, some carrying big long saws, others old lunch pails, but the most unnerving one of all was one of what appeared to be the ghost of an Indian warming himself by the embers of my fire right outside my tent! This was too much!

I packed away the camera and the laptop, and with Jet continued on down the trail as fast as we could. But as we moved I could see that the weather was rapidly changing. Dark clouds were pushing in and the wind was picking up rapidly. I didn't want to stay in the horrid place one second longer than I had to but in my haste I tripped on a tree root that was sticking out of the ground and twisted my ankle. It wasn't a bad sprain but enough to keep me from moving any further. So with the weather turning sour and night falling, I reluctantly set up my tent, and against my better judgment I set up the trap camera.

I finished setting up the tent, and moments later heard thunder off in the distance. Jet, who was constantly at my side, needed no coaxing to get in. I zipped up the door just as rain began to fall. Soon the wind was absolutely howling down the trail and a full-blown electrical storm was in progress. Thunder and lightning were almost simultaneous, indicating the storm was directly overhead; it was an incredible display of light and sound. And all the while I could see the trap camera flashing, taking pictures every few moments. I didn't get much sleep that night; I may have dozed off around three in the morning, when the storm subsided. I awoke a few hours later as the sun was coming up. This time I went out and grabbed the trap camera and plugged it into my laptop right away. It indicated that over 100 pictures had been taken during the storm.

This time it captured ghostly images that looked like military supply wagons, some of soldiers marching, others of Cavalry racing down the trail, still more of sheep herders, and my old friend the Indian was back. I packed up and headed down the trail as swiftly as my sore ankle would carry me, and even though there was nothing in these images that appeared threatening, I still didn't want to spend another night on the trail. About noon I made it back to my starting point near Franklin Lake.

I called my uncle and asked him for a ride. In about a half hour he picked me up and we were soon back at Pike Lake. "How was your hike?" he asked.

I explained in great detail the hike and the images I had captured with the trap camera. He looked at me kinda skeptically. So as soon as I was inside I plugged in my laptop and hooked it up to the camera. And much to my surprise, no images appeared on my laptop. I checked the connections but to no avail; the entire camera was blank. Somehow it all had been erased. I felt foolish now that all my evidence was lost and I had nothing to support my claims.

I'm not sure if my uncle and aunt ever believed me, but I didn't come away from my adventure without learning something, the first being I will be back again to hike and explore, though I probably won't bring a trap camera next time. And maybe I won't come back right away. I think next year I will go down to Florida with my brother. He is thinking of going down there to start a nature preserve for oversized sea cows; he plans on calling it "Habitat for Huge Manatees." But that's a different story.

The Night of the Witch

There are two rules that sailors on the Great Lakes must adhere to. Rule #1: Do not sail on the lakes in November. Rule #2: If you must sail on the lakes in November, always remember Rule #1.

As a young man I spent the early years of the 1900s crewing on a small wooden steamer that spent most of its time on Lake Superior. We sailed a semi-regular route that we covered about every two weeks or so, carrying just about anything and everything: mail, freight, machinery and even passengers to scheduled stops all around the lake. Now the rules about not sailing on the lakes in November applied to all the lakes but it especially held true for Superior. Our ship's captain, with more than forty years of experience on the Great Lakes, would normally not violate this rule. However, rules, through choice or fate, are often broken.

It was the second week of October 1913 and the trees around the lake were well into shedding their leaves. Much cooler temperatures were also making their presence known, and Superior itself had taken on a decidedly more sinister feel. We were at our dock in Sault Ste. Marie, which is on the St. Mary's River leading to Whitefish Bay. We had thoughts leaning more towards mooring the ship for the next several months to ride out the winter, when our captain came down the pier with a look on his face that was a mixture of anger and fear. He gave us orders to prepare the ship for sailing, explaining that the company had ordered us back out onto the lake. One of our sister vessels had blown a steam pipe and lost all power, and the winds had pushed her aground on a deadly saw-tooth reef near Eagle River, Michigan. We were to assist with her salvage and complete her delivery circuit of Lake Superior.

Salvage of our sister ship took longer than expected due to ever-increasingly rough seas and generally lousy weather. It was the end of October by the time we got her cargo transferred to our vessel. Leaving our crippled sister in care of a salvage company, we set sail on our normal route to complete the deliveries. Before we had left, however, I had overheard the captain of the stranded ship speaking to our captain. I didn't hear everything he said but I distinctly heard him tell our captain, "It was the witch that grounded us. She tried to send us to the bottom and had we not stranded on this reef, she would have. Beware, for she is hungry this year."

Our captain didn't say anything but I could clearly see him slowly nod his head in understanding. Despite the ever-increasing seas and almost constant rain we made good time to Duluth and Isle Royale, but it was the second week of November by the time we put into Thunder Bay, where we were delayed for forty-eight hours. With each passing hour the lake seemed to become more restless, as did our captain. Our last stop before turning for home was Red Rock on the northern shore of Superior. We unloaded the last of the cargo and immediately set sail across the lake for Whitefish Bay.

Captain ordered the engine to full speed, when the chief engineer complained that maintaining this speed was hard on his engines. The captain simply acknowledged his concerns but did nothing to alter the ship's speed. About two thirds the way across the lake the skies turned to almost a solid gray and the water suddenly grew calm. I was in the wheelhouse when this occurred, and as the seas calmed so did the demeanor of our captain. He kept the ship's speed up and sat in his chair, sipping tea as he stared out the back window of the pilothouse as if watching for something. When I asked him what he was watching for, his reply sent chills down my spine.

"The witch is coming. She wants to catch us on the open lake," he said.

An hour later he summoned me back to the wheelhouse. When I got there he handed me the ship's log books. "Take care of these and don't let anything happen to them," he told me.

Being on Superior in November was enough to make a sailor nervous, but after the captain gave me the ship's logs, I was almost in a panic. And if that wasn't enough, as I turned to leave the pilothouse, he said, "Get your life jacket on and tell the crew to do likewise."

As soon as I stepped out onto the exposed deck I could see that the lake had once again turned violent, as if somewhere someone had thrown a switch. I made it to my room in the crew quarters, telling everyone I saw along the way to put on their life jackets. I found my jacket, and just then a series of violent waves rocked the ship. We had sailed straight into the teeth of a horrific storm that seemed to have materialized out of nowhere. The wind began to howl as snow and freezing rain pummeled the ship. We were being tossed about in the tempest, and every one of us thought our time was at hand.

Suddenly a ray of hope, the lighthouse at Whitefish Point, came into view. All we had to do was make the bay and our chances of survival would increase dramatically. But just as salvation seemed at hand, it was cruelly snatched away. The ship's steering gear let go, the rudder would no longer answer the helm, and we were adrift and at the mercy of the relentless storm. The captain, meanwhile, remained unusually calm. He ordered the distress flag to be raised, hoping it would be sighted by the lifesaving station at Whitefish Point, but even so there was no way for us to get off of our wildly drifting vessel. As fortune or fate would have it, we were pushed onto the shoals about a mile from the point. It was on this precarious perch the captain ordered the lifeboat launched and everyone into it.

The entire crew had jumped into the lifeboat, and the first mate held a rope that was tied to the ship's rail. The captain was still in the wheelhouse and we yelled for him to join us in the lifeboat. A moment later he emerged with a fire ax in his hand and a look of sheer determination on his face. He headed straight for us, and as we stared in disbelief, he got to the rail and swung the ax, severing the rope holding the lifeboat to the ship. Seconds later we were swept away from the doomed vessel with our captain still on board.

As the wind carried us towards the beach we could see our ship suddenly break free of the shoal and begin drifting out into the open lake. We watched the captain climb on top of the wheelhouse. The last we could see of him, he was hanging onto a cable and waving the ax in defiance. About a half mile from shore we met the crew of the Whitefish Point lifesaving station; they had rowed out to meet us and took our boat in tow. By the time we reached the shore we were all drenched to the skin and shivering violently. They took us to the lighthouse, where the keeper's wife gave us blankets and hot coffee. We huddled near the fireplace all night as sleet and hail beat against the shuttered windows, sounding very much like boney fingers clawing against the glass. All through the night the wind howled and screeched in a most unearthly, bone-chilling manner, often times rising to a wicked crescendo that sent chills down the spines of even the most stout-hearted of us.

Shortly after dawn the storm broke and relative calm returned to the skies. Having dried off, we donned our coats and went out to see what, if anything, remained of our ship and our captain. Even though the storm had passed, huge breakers still pounded the shore. There was flotsam from at least a dozen ships scattered up and down the beach for as far one could see in either direction. We picked through the debris, and eventually we found several pieces of a ship's name board. When we pieced together the splintered remains, we could make out *SS Carl Spencer*, the name of our ship.

With our ship and captain obviously gone we boarded a train to take us back to Sault Ste. Marie. The company said they would send a ship for us but we declined, for none of us were willing to go back out onto the lake. About halfway back I thought of the log books the captain had given me and pulled them out. On the five days prior to the storm, the captain had not written any of the normal log entries. Instead on every page was scrawled, "The witch is coming." This was indeed chilling to read. Apparently he believed that the bloodlust of the witch would not be satisfied unless she took our ship and crew to eternity. The captain bravely sacrificed himself in order to save the crew.

In honor of his selfless act I decided to write a tribute to him for the final log, crediting him for saving our lives. But when I turned to the last page, already written there in the captain's handwriting was the following entry: "Ship wrecked at Whitefish Point, crew safe, captain lost with ship." Had our captain struck some unearthly deal with the Witch of November in order to save his crew? Or had he tricked her into taking an almost empty vessel to the cold dark depths of Superior, making her victory a hollow one at best? There was no way any of us would ever know. In spring, most of the crew and I returned to sail once again on Superior. However, it was with a newfound respect, and with the understanding that not one of us who survived that day would ever again set sail on the lake in the month of November.

The Wanderer

I've often wondered where the roots of a ghost story lay. Most that I have heard are passed down from one generation to the next, usually becoming distorted with each retelling. Others are rooted in hearsay, pieced together from several "not so credible" witnesses that claim that they know someone who knows someone that was actually involved.

Yet the scariest I think by far are the ones that you experience first hand. This is a story that began perhaps a century ago but I encountered it only last September.

Last fall I was staying at a resort on Eagle Lake. I got up early in the morning like I usually do and took a walk in the predawn light until I reached another lake. It was here on Dollar Lake Road that I encountered something so shocking that at first I didn't want to tell anyone about it.

I collect old camping lanterns and, since it was still dark, I lit one to take with me as I headed off through the woods on an old dirt road. As I moved through the trees the lantern cast an eerie light in the chilly dark of the morning. I remember thinking to myself that if anyone saw me they would be "freaked out" by this strange light floating through the woods. I have to admit, I thought it was pretty funny. I wandered around in the woods until I found a trail that led back out to the road. About this time a low ground fog began to roll through the trees, and in a few moments the visibility was cut down to only a few yards.

Reaching Dollar Lake Road, I went down the road leading back to the resort. About halfway there I suddenly heard a noise behind me; turning back I saw a single light bobbing in the fog. I stepped off the road, figuring it was a car or a truck or something with one burned-out headlight and that I would just move off the road and let them pass. As the light got closer I distinctly heard the sound of horse hooves on the asphalt. At this point I was thinking it was some lost Amish guy. Then suddenly, an old man dressed in ragged nineteenth century bed clothes emerged from the fog. In his out-stretched hand he held a lit barn lantern, staggering down the road as if he would collapse at any moment. He turned his head to look at me and it was at this point I saw that he had no eyes at all, just hollow sockets void of any sign of life. I stepped back in horror at the shocking sight that was just inches from me, and I lost my footing in the soft gravel of the roadside and fell down.

Before I could digest this horrendous apparition, two harnessed horses emerged in tandem from the fog. They too were clearly long dead, as I could see the white of bone sticking through their battered coats in several places. But what came next shocked me most of all.

Attached to these two pathetic creatures was an old, carriage-style hearse, with a torch burning at each corner. As it rolled slowly by me, I clearly saw through the glass sides a shiny black coffin illuminated by a single candle on each side. I watched in utter disbelief as the macabre parade continued on down the road and once again disappeared into the fog from which it had come. The steady clip-clop of the hoof beats and the torches on the hearse both faded away at about the same time. Scrambling to my feet I quickly found the driveway and made my way back to my room at the resort. Somewhat stunned by these events, I couldn't find the words to describe to anyone what I had seen. Until now I had told almost no one.

So several weeks ago when we were up here I stopped by the library but could find nothing in their collection that pertained to what I had seen. Going outside I encountered an older, heavyset woman with silver hair soliciting donations for the VA. I gave her a dollar, and as a second thought asked her if she had lived in the area long.

"My whole life," she told me. I then told her about what I had seen on Dollar Lake Road. She didn't seem too surprised. "So you've seen it?" she asked matter of factly. I nodded in response.

"Not a lot of people witness that," she began to explain. "In the seventy-five years I've lived here I have only seen it once. But I saw it on Township Road near Duck Lake in 1957. Came out of the morning fog just like you said."

She proceeded to tell me the story of a man that once lived in Eagle River by the name of Graff Morey. "My grandparents knew him well. He was a swindler and a bureaucratic thug that tried to trick them into selling their farm to him. Their place was on the north side of Eagle River. Their barn still stands on the east side of Highway 45 just outside of town. Morey found out that the C&NW was going to extend their tracks north through town and on up to Watersmeet in Michigan and beyond, and he knew they would pay big money for my grandparents' farm, which stood on the proposed route. He tried to force Granddad into signing over the land to him at a fraction of what it was worth. Granddad was one of the few people that stood up to Morey and would not sell to him. When he couldn't get my grandparents to sell to him he began to swindle other people out of their land. He bit off more than he could chew, however, when he came up against the small band of Indians that claimed Duck Lake as their home. Morey found some old forgotten treaty from decades past and used it to force the Indians off their land. The Army was called in to evict them, and as they filed past a grinning Graff Morey, the tribe's holy man shook a rain stick at him and said that upon Morey's death he would never find rest and was doomed to wander the land, blind, forever searching for his grave.

"Graff Morey, of course, laughed at this. But years later, upon his death bed late one night in his home on the land near Duck

Lake that he had forced the Indians off of, with a doctor and several others in attendance, Morey suddenly sat up in his bed and gasped and at the same moment everyone in the room heard what sounded like a drumbeat accompanied by an Indian chant coming from seemingly nowhere yet everywhere in the room. Without warning, Morey screamed, dug his fingers into his eye sockets, gouged out his own eyes and then fell back dead upon his covers.

"Still in his bed clothes he was loaded into a coffin and placed in an elaborate horse-drawn hearse. While the men in attendance, all of whom had witnessed Graff Morey's final moments, stood nearby and argued about who would drive the body to the cemetery in nearby Eagle River, a thick, glowing fog enveloped the hearse.

"The arguing stopped when everyone heard the unmistakable sound of the coffin lid opening, then the sound of someone getting down out of the hearse. Suddenly, a hand reached out of the fog and grasped a lit lantern that was sitting on the ground nearby. The men, now silenced with fear, watched as the light seemingly floated through the fog to the front of the horses. Next, the light moved slowly down the road, leading the hearse off. No one dared try to stop it.

"Word spread through the small community, and a search for the missing hearse, horses and the deceased Graff Morey began the next morning. Months of searching turned up nothing, and eventually the search was called off. Years later people began to report seeing Graff Morey leading the hearse through a fog, apparently in search of the cemetery."

With that the old woman excused herself and left me alone in front of the library to ponder the story.

So now I tell you this: if you decide to take a walk in the early morning and you find yourself in a thick, glowing fog and hear the sound of tired hoof beats, you may want to step off the road. But do not fear, it will not harm you. It's only Graff Morey trying to find his grave.

The Dark Secret of Willow Creek Coal Mine

Somewhere east of Eagle River, deep inside the shadowy Nicolet National Forest, stands the remains of what was once the old Willow Creek Coal Mine. Abandoned in the late 1950s, Willow Creek Coal Mine once had one of the richest veins of coal in Vilas County, producing on average five tons of pure anthracite coal a day. Today the mine sits silent, its gaping dark entrance foreboding. Its exact location is known by only a few and it's visited by even less.

Well, a month or so ago, the two Weaver brothers, who live on a farm on the edge of the forest, were out hunting in the woods. After several hours of traipsing through the pines they realized that they were lost. And to make matters worse it was getting late, the weather was closing in, and before they knew it, it began to rain. Now having grown up in Vilas County, these young men knew enough to know that they needed to find their way out or find suitable shelter fast. In the waning daylight hours they spotted a cave opening in the distance. Running through the ever-increasing showers they reached the cave and ran inside, just as a loud thunderclap exploded above the trees directly over their heads. This was followed by a torrential downpour.

"Boy, we made it just in time," one of the boys said.

The other boy nodded. Both boys were shivering.

"We need to get a fire going."

Like I said before, these boys, having grown up in Vilas County, may not have had enough sense to take a compass into the woods, but they did have enough sense to bring along some basic survival gear that included matches. Finding some old boards and other assorted scraps of wood they soon had a small fire going in the cave entrance. By this time it was completely dark. The boys sat near the fire trying to keep warm as the rain and lightning continued steadily.

"Mom is gonna kill us," one of the boys said.

"No," the other replied. "Mom is gonna freak out, and Dad is gonna kill us."

The other boy nodded in agreement.

While all this was going on, back at the boys' home on the farm that bordered the forest, their mother stared out of the kitchen window into the pouring rain. Supper was approaching and she knew her sons were overdue.

"What's the matter, dear?" her husband asked as he entered the kitchen.

"Boys are late," she said. "They knew Granddad was coming for dinner and they are never late when he comes."

"I'd better go look," the father said.

The father was just getting into his truck when Granddad pulled up.

"Where you off to, Bill?" he asked.

"Boys went hunting down by Willow Creek and are late," he replied.

"Willow Creek?" Granddad asked with a noticeable change in demeanor.

"Yep."

Granddad's face went noticeably pale. He jumped into the passenger side of the pick up.

"Drive!" he demanded. "I know where they are."

"Should I get my gun?" Bill asked.

"Wouldn't do you any good," Granddad replied.

After an hour or so the boys had warmed up and their coats were now dry enough to put back on.

"Where do you think we are?"

The second boy didn't answer as he stared down into the blackness of the cave.

"I keep hearing noises," he said. "Sounds almost like someone crying."

"I hear it too. Shall we go look?"

One of the boys picked up a branch out of the fire to use as a torch. Holding it high to gain as much light as possible they cautiously moved deeper into the cave. The farther in they went into the cave the more pronounced the weeping sound became.

"I'm not going any deeper," one of the boys said with a noticeable quiver in his voice.

"I agree," replied the other. "Let's get out of here."

At that very moment the makeshift torch they were carrying was slapped out of the boy's hand and went out. Then the weeping sound grew louder, as if it was within an arm's length of the two boys.

Suddenly a bolt of lightning stuck a tree right outside the cave entrance. In the flash that illuminated the cave for an instant, the boys could see a woman standing right in front of them in what appeared to be a wedding dress stained black with coal dust.

"RUN!" the boys shouted in unison.

They stumbled and tripped as they tried to make their way back to the entrance. For a moment they were lost and disoriented in the pitch blackness. Suddenly the brilliant light of a Coleman lantern filled the cave and they heard the familiar voice of their grandfather.

"Boys, this way!" he shouted.

They ran towards the light and plowed right into their dad.

"DAD!" they shouted in unison. "There's a ghost back there."

"It's not a ghost," Granddad said as he stepped past the boys and placed himself between them and the deeper part of the cave.

"It's much worse; it's a banshee."

No sooner had those words escaped his lips when a most horrific, bone-chilling, terrifying, ear-shattering scream came from deep inside the cave. Everyone except Granddad was startled beyond intelligent thought. Granddad held his ground, clutching the lantern high in the air so it shone as deep into the abyss as it could.

"It won't come into the light," he said, "but we need to get out of here now."

The banshee screamed again, except this time it screamed the last name of the family. "WEAVER WEAVER WEAVER!!!"

Again Granddad held his ground. And reiterated what he said before. "MOVE NOW!" he demanded.

The boys and their father ran out of the cave, and Granddad backed out, all the while keeping the lantern held high. Once outside, he gathered everyone together a fair distance from the opening.

"Everyone all right?" he asked.

A chorus of "Yes" came back.

"What was that thing?" Dad asked.

"A banshee," Granddad explained. "But let's go home. I'll explain everything."

After dinner Granddad sat down on the porch and lit his pipe. Everyone took seats nearby, and without being prompted, Granddad began to explain.

"First of all, that is not a cave; that opening is all that remains of the Willow Creek Coal Mine. Back in the 1950s, when I was just out of high school, I worked there as a coal miner for a few years.

"The head miner at Willow Creek was a guy named Jim Fellows. He had been dating a rather eccentric young woman from Eagle River for a while and they decided to get married. On the day of the wedding word came that there had been a partial collapse at the mine and several men were missing. Jim left the ceremony right after the 'I do's' and went to the mine to lead a search party.

About half hour after Jim and several miners entered the mine, a bigger cave-in occurred. Well, Jim's new bride was outside, still in her wedding dress, when the second cave-in happened. She screamed and ran into the mine. We found her about a quarter mile deep in the mine. She had been clawing at the mountain of coal that had fallen. She was dead, choked to death on the coal dust from the cave-in.

"In the weeks that followed we worked to reopen the collapsed tunnels. During that time we recovered most of the bodies. We buried Jim and his new bride next to each other in the Eagle River cemetery. Shortly after that, miners began reporting hearing weeping sounds, which over time grew into miners hearing their names called, and finally the appearance of the banshee. As near as we could figure it was the tortured soul of Jim Fellows's wife. Somehow she blamed the miners for her husband's death and decided to stay in this world to torment us. 'Long about 1955, the owners closed the mine because they couldn't keep any miners. One encounter with the banshee was enough to make a person seek employment elsewhere. A few guys even died of fright. I was one of the last people to set foot inside. I took a crew in and we dynamited the tunnel, collapsing all but the last 150 feet or so. After the dust settled we could clearly see her standing in the shadow of the cave entrance, beckoning us to her, shrieking our names. Until today, I had not set foot in that mine since we dynamited it."

With that Granddad tamped out his pipe on the bottom of his shoe and then zipped it up in his tobacco pouch. Standing up he said, "Goodnight," stepped off the porch and in a moment was in his truck, headed home.

It is unknown how long the widow of Jim Fellows will remain in Willow Creek Coal Mine or what unearthly desire for revenge drives her tortured spirit. What is known is that the Weaver brothers will have no immediate desire to hunt in that part of the woods any time soon. And if you ever find yourself lost in that part of the Nicolet National Forest and the only shelter you can find is an old abandoned mine, you just might want to take your chances out in the weather rather than in the clutches of the Willow Creek Banshee.

The Witch of Willow Corners

Everyone has a place that they like to "escape" to, a place your thoughts default to when normal life begins to wear you down, when your boss or your teachers or your customers have succeeded in pushing you to your breaking point. You dream of the one place that makes life bearable again. And you dream of getting back there as soon as you can. I have such a place, tranquil, quiet and peaceful. I never would have imagined that formerly it was a place dark and sinister where unspeakable horror once existed.

If you take what is today Highway 70, west of Eagle River, you will eventually come to the intersection of Highway 155. Decades ago this junction was named for a grove of willow trees that stood at this intersection, giving the little town its name of Willow Corners. It is here, in this quiet little place far off the beaten path, that our story takes place.

Deep in the wood of willows on the southwest corner of the junction on the opposite side from the town, stood an old log home that had been there well over 100 years. A woman named Mattie who once lived as a beachcomber on Lake Superior's Isle Royale moved into the home around 1920 and lived there with her only companion, a cat with jet-black fir and strange yellow eyes. Mattie kept to herself, and most of the townsfolk were fine with this arrangement. Seems most people were afraid of her, with rumors of strange lights emitting from her house and eerie unearthly sounds at all hours of the night keeping the curious away. Not to mention that stray cats and dogs would not tread near her house or even into the grove of trees that surrounded it.

Well, time passed as it has a tendency to do and as it did the town began to grow. More people came to live in Willow Corners, drawn in by the booming lumber industry and the good paying jobs that accompanied it. Soon the spread of the little burg began to encroach on the willows that surrounded Mattie's house. The town elders began to talk of kicking Mattie out of her home and clearing the land for a small airport. A town meeting was held and it was decided to offer Mattie a tidy sum for her property in hopes of convincing her to move.

Early on a Monday morning, four men selected by the town elders were sent to Mattie's house in the willow grove to make the offer. And if she refused, these four were instructed to use "other" methods to force her off the property. By noon that day the men had not returned and no one had seen them since they were last seen entering the woods that surrounded Mattie's home. Wild rumors began to circulate among the town folk as evening came and went with no sign of the four men. As the next day passed, the town elders tried to get more men to go looking for the first, but no one would volunteer. Finally at dusk on the third day, one of the men came staggering out of the grove and into the town. People gasped when they saw him. When he had gone into the grove he was a young, strong man of twenty-four years of age. Now, his dark hair had turned pure white and he looked like he had aged sixty years.

He stumbled as he walked and his body trembled as if he had experienced some unspeakable, unearthly horror. A crowd gathered around him to hear what he had to say. All he could do was mumble, "Dead, dead, they're all dead," over and over. His eyes stared straight ahead, not looking at anyone or even acknowledging those around him. Suddenly he stopped his trembling and without a sound he fell flat on the earth like a giant oak felled by a lumberjack. No one had to say it; everyone knew the man was dead.

A gasp went through the crowd. Cries of "Burn the witch!" were heard. A mob formed and with lit torches they went into the willow grove to Mattie's log home. One man hurled a torch through a window, another threw one on the roof and a third man landed one on the porch. Flames spread as Mattie's black cat leaped from the broken window onto the burning porch and then sprang onto the roof. It sat up there hissing menacingly as the flames flared up around it. However, the cat was not hissing at the encroaching flames, it was clearly hissing at the mob. Suddenly the roof collapsed into the house, taking the cat with it.

"No one could survive that," someone in the crowd said. People breathed a sigh of relief, when without warning a column of intense flame shot high into the sky, followed by wicked, maniacal laughter coming from somewhere within the inferno. The crowd of people all ran from the woods. Early the next morning after a bright sun rose in the sky, about half of the mob from the night before returned to the smoldering remains of Mattie's former home. There was nothing left; everything was ashes. No remains of Mattie, the three missing henchmen or the cat were found. Later that week, the town gathered to bury the young man that had returned from the willow grove and died in the center of Main Street. The town preacher concluded the graveside service and asked for a moment of silence. Just as he did the crowd heard a menacing hiss from only a few yards away.

Everyone turned to see Mattie's black cat, with its yellow eyes glowing, perched defiantly on top of the largest gravestone in the cemetery. At that very moment lightning from out of a clear blue sky struck the headstone of the man they came to bury and shattered it into a million pieces. Then seemingly out of thin air Mattie's raspy voice was heard. "*I will be back to seek my revenge on the night of the harvest moon.*"

Panic ensued, since the fall harvest was only a week away and a full moon was expected. Some people packed up everything they had and left Willow Corners forever. Others vowed to stay and fight whatever the witch might have in store for them.

One full day before the expected harvest moon, Germain, the old Indian medicine man from a nearby tribe, came into town. He went to the town elders and explained that he had heard about the witch and that he could help. The town folk agreed to let him try. The medicine man set himself up on one side of the crossroads across from the grove where Mattie's log house once stood. He built a fire, and just after the sun set, he began to chant some strange Indian incantations and at the same time threw small bits of sage brush and other herbs into the flame. An owl landed in the tree nearby and screeched out as if in warning, and a wolf howled from the nearby woods as a low ground fog rolled out of the trees behind him.

The moon appeared in the sky and by its light the townspeople that gathered to watch could see a dark figure sailing through the sky from the west. A second later the unmistakable hiss of Mattie's black cat was heard from across the road. Within moments the flying figure approached the crossroads then suddenly landed about halfway across the road. It was Mattie, looking very much like a witch from Grimm's fairy tales. Dark pointed hat, black cape and clutching a broom with her hissing cat circling her feet as she stood there. She pointed a boney figure at the crowd of people and said in her raspy voice, "FOOLS!! That medicine man can't help you!"

Yet she paced the road back and forth as the medicine man chanted. Something was keeping her from coming into the town. The Indian began to chant more loudly and threw more sage into the fire. It flamed up higher and Mattie threw her arms over her face and screamed, obviously affected by the medicine man's efforts. Finally she mounted her broom, her cat jumped on the back, and as she flew away she threatened, "I'll be back one day! I will have my revenge!!!"

The town folk were very grateful to the Indian medicine man, and even though there was no evidence that Mattie would ever return, every harvest moon he would come back, perform the ritual and keep the witch at bay. Years passed and eventually the medicine man passed away.

The town folk, in an effort to keep Mattie away, carved a fifteen-foot likeness of the Indian, and today he stands defiantly at the corner, watching for the witch. The little runway the town elders wanted to build was completed, but failed a few years later. Today a school and a baseball field sit on the site. The only known evidence that the airport ever existed is a single photograph on the wall of a café on the edge of town. And, oh yes, to show the overwhelming gratitude of the townspeople to the medicine man that saved Willow Corners, they renamed their city in a way so he would never be forgotten. They bestowed the title "Saint" to his name, and the little town that was founded as Willow Corners so long ago is known today as St. Germain.

Tonight at Duffy's Tavern

Everyone knows that Chicago is the railroad capital of the Midwest. Just about every railroad that ever existed at one time or another was somehow connected to the city of Chicago. One of biggest, which only recently became a fallen flag, was the Chicago and Northwestern. The C&NW had tracks all over the Midwest. One of the northernmost stops on the line is the town of Eagle River, Wisconsin. Once a bustling scene of activity with a constant flow of passengers and freight, today the Eagle River depot is only a shadow of its former self. Of all the buildings that were once associated with the railroad, all that remains standing, currently in use as a small museum, is the passenger depot itself. About a quarter mile to the west of the old depot is the headwaters of the mighty Wisconsin River. It is near this junction of the rail line and the river where a small bar called Duffy's Tavern once stood. Sheamus (pronounced "Shaymus") McDuffy was the owner, and it was here he could be found most nights of the week tending bar.

McDuffy, a first-generation immigrant, had come to America from Ireland with his parents in the 1880s as a lad of seventeen. Full of adventure and the ideology possessed by only a young man, Sheamus McDuffy soon set out on his own to see America. Bidding his parents farewell, he boarded an empty box car in the rail yards that stood near his parents' modest dwelling in New York City. In the matter of a decade or so of "ridin' the rails," McDuffy had crisscrossed the country several times and eventually found his way to Eagle River, where he found work as a barkeep in run-down tavern called the Eagle River Saloon, which most people called the Eagle River Spittoon due to the fact that the owner chewed tobacco almost constantly and didn't seem to own a clean shirt. Needless to say, it was not a popular or profitable establishment. McDuffy found he liked the area and, having grown up on the shore of the Irish Sea, discovered the lengthy Wisconsin winters did not bother him. Within a year the owner of the tavern passed away, and since he had no kin, he willed the bar to Sheamus McDuffy. Finding he had a mind for business, McDuffy soon had the place turned around and profitable. Under its new ownership and name, Duffy's Tavern, business thrived. For the next four decades, "Duffy's" became a staple of life in Eagle River.

Sometime in the late 1920s a new patron began to become a regular at Duffy's. James Morgan, or "Morgan," as he liked to be called, was also an Irishman and a retired Chicago Police officer. While still a cop, he had been sent to Eagle River to recover and escort the charred remains of notorious gangster John "Johnny Rotten" Rattan back to Chicago. He found that he liked the area, and having had his fill after twenty-seven years on the beat in the Windy City, he retired from police work and took a job with the Chicago and Northwestern in Eagle River. After his first day on the job as an engineer, Morgan went into Duffy's and became a regular.

Now Morgan, like Sheamus McDuffy, was a proud Irishman, and as true Irishmen do, Morgan and McDuffy had a tendency to butt heads. They argued about anything and everything, mostly about muskie fishing, but it really didn't matter what, anything was fair game. The weather, types of ale, who was a better hunter, where the best fishing spots were, which was colder—the North Sea or the Irish Sea, etc., etc., etc. Most people's first impressions when they saw the two argue was that they could not stand each other. This could not be further from the truth, for they regularly went fishing and hunting together and were the best of friends.

The two men even had a standing bet. Each Friday night "the

400" was scheduled to arrive with the "Sportsman's Special" promptly at 9:00 p.m. Several times a week, the C&NW railroad ran a passenger train from Chicago to the Upper Peninsula of Michigan, making stops in Milwaukee, Green Bay and Eagle River before reaching its final destination. They named it the 400 because the route took approximately 400 minutes to complete. On Friday nights they nicknamed the route the Sportsman's Special because people who liked to fish, hunt or camp in the Eagle River area took that train up for the weekend, and James Morgan, who was regularly the engineer of the 400 on Friday nights, took great personal pride in making sure the train was always on time.

According to their wager, if it was on time, McDuffy had to buy a round of drinks for everyone in the bar. If it was late, Morgan had to buy the round. Funny thing was the 400 was almost never late, and week after week, McDuffy was forced to buy a free round for his patrons. The winter of 1932 to 1933 was as bitter and cold as anyone could remember, yet the nine o'clock Friday night arrival of the 400 was always on time. Finally, in early 1933, a blizzard hit Vilas County on a Friday and McDuffy was sure that this was the night he would finally win the bet. The bar was quiet and strangely there was no sign of Morgan as the nine o'clock hour approached. Everyone's eyes were on the Seth Thomas clock that hung on the wall, watching as the minutes ticked away.

Sure enough, as the appointed time came and went, there was no train or even a whistle indicating the arrival of the 400. Along about an hour after the appointed time, a lone figure could be seen making his way to Duffy's Tavern. With a blast of cold air the figure stepped inside.

"Morgan!" McDuffy exclaimed with a smile. "What's with the 400 tonight?"

"Late," was all Morgan said. Stomping the snow off his feet, he stopped at the fire to warm himself. After chasing the chill off, Morgan then made his way to his favorite stool at the bar.

"Come to settle my bet," Morgan said as he sat down. "Drinks are on me."

A cheer went up from the room. McDuffy poured a deep glass of Irish ale and set it in front of Morgan, who was busy studying his railroad watch, then grinning from ear to ear in sheer satisfaction, McDuffy proceeded to pass out drinks to the rest of the patrons.

About thirty minutes or so later another figure came into the bar out of the bitter cold. It was Jack Winters, the local station master. He moved to fireplace to warm up. While he stood there with his back to the room McDuffy came up and offered him a drink.

"I have some bad news, Sheamus," Winters said.

"What's that?" McDuffy asked.

"The 400 wrecked at Mosquito Creek tonight," Winters said quietly.

Continuing, he explained, "It looks like it ran into an open switch; it went onto the siding at high speed and stuck the track car from Three Lakes. Almost everyone was killed."

"The 400 is Morgan's train," McDuffy replied. "Who was the engineer tonight?"

"Morgan," Winters replied. "He's dead along with the rest of the train crew and most of the passengers.

"Morgan is right there," McDuffy said, turning and pointing at Morgan's favorite place at the bar. McDuffy suddenly gasped as he saw the now-empty bar stool. The empty glass of Irish ale had foam running down from the rim, as if someone had just finished drinking from it and set it down on the bar just seconds before. The two men hurried over to the now-vacant seat. Next to the empty glass sat the money to cover the round of drinks he had ordered, and on top of that sat Morgan's railroad watch, its crystal smashed and the hands now forever stuck at 8:35 p.m.

"He would have made it on time," McDuffy said. Picking up the watch, Morgan's St. Christopher medal dangled at the end of the chain.

"They found him in the wreckage of the cab, his hand still on the brake lever," Winters said, staring at the broken time piece.

McDuffy caught the medal in his other hand. "The patron saint of travelers," he said, looking at the image of St. Christopher. "I guess you don't need this anymore. Your travels are now over, old friend."

"I think he wanted his journey to end tonight at Duffy's Tavern," Winters said. "That is where they have ended every Friday night for the last eight years."

With that, McDuffy hung the watch over the bar. Later on he hung a framed picture of the 400 with Morgan waving from the cab of the steam engine next to it, and above that hung James Morgan's two favorite fishing poles that Morgan's widow gave to McDuffy, saying that he would have wanted Sheamus to have them.

Duffy's Tavern remained a staple to life in Eagle River for many more years. Long before the 400 stopped running, Sheamus McDuffy died at a ripe old age.

The tavern that stood so long as Duffy's caught fire and burned to the ground, and eventually the descendents of Sheamus McDuffy donated the land to the city. Today it is a city park.

It is said that on the anniversary of the train wreck, a case of Irish ale will mysteriously appear on a park bench near the spot of Morgan's favorite bar stool, free for the taking.

As for Sheamus McDuffy and James Morgan, rumor has it that both of their remains were cremated and scattered in the channel that connects Eagle and Rice Lakes. Strangely enough, today there are two crusty old snapping turtles that on occasion can be seen in this area. No one knows why, but for as long as anyone can remember, they have been referred to as "Morgan" and "McDuffy."

The Last Run of the "400"

I don't know how many of you have ever spent the winter in northern Wisconsin. If you have, then you know it gets cold in the fall, the snow comes early, and it stays too long for most folks. There are long stretches where the temperature hovers between bitter cold and "you've got to be kidding me." Even the sun gets up late and goes to bed early during the deepest part of the Wisconsin winter. In this darkest part of the year only the truly hardy make it a point to spend time outdoors hunting, skiing, ice fishing and, of course, snowmobiling. Upper Wisconsin is teeming with snowmobile trails, most of which follow the former railroad right-of-ways that once crisscrossed the land.

As the story goes, there was a young lady named Sarah that loved to snowmobile. Sarah lived on a lake east of Eagle River with her parents and her older sister. Along with her dad she would race along the well-groomed trails that covered the area. One day they decided to take a quick trip to Three Lakes, which was about ten miles to the south. Around noon they left and about an hour later they arrived in Three Lakes. Well, as these things go, Dad and Sarah ended up spending too much time in the shops and visiting friends and it was late afternoon before they began their trip back home. Sarah, on her smaller red snowmobile, led them out of town as the sun began to settle in the western sky. They got about halfway home when Sarah's sled suddenly sputtered then stalled. She coasted to the side of the trail, and Dad pulled up beside her.

"What's wrong?" he asked.

Sarah shrugged. "Dunno."

Dad got off his snowmobile and looked over Sarah's machine; finally he pulled open the gas cap.

"No gas," he said.

It was decided that Sarah, being old enough, would stay with her sled and Dad would go get some gas. It was dusk when Dad left, promising he would be back as soon as possible. Since Sarah was well dressed for being outdoors she was not concerned too much about the cold. Soon the sun was gone from the horizon and stars began to appear overhead. Sarah lit the flare her Dad had left her to warn other snowmobilers and placed it in the snow alongside the sled. Sitting on the seat, she thought it unusual that there was no one else out on the trail this night. It was at this very moment she heard something strange. Far off to the south she heard the unmistakable sound of train whistle.

"Why was this strange?" you might ask. Well, Sarah knew that the nearest railroad tracks were down in Rhinelander. This was much too far away for sound to travel even on a clear and cold Wisconsin night. Suddenly she heard the sound again, but this time it was closer. Peering south down the trail in the direction of the sound she could not help but get a little nervous. As she watched down the trail she heard it yet again. This time it was closer still and now she could see a headlight! This was beyond weird! There was no place for her to go, so she sat on her snowmobile and watched the light get closer and closer to her. And now there were other sounds. The clanking of an engine was plainly heard, along with the puffing sound that a steam train makes. Quite frankly, Sarah was paralyzed with fear and could not move. Suddenly she saw it. An old steam engine roared into sight, dragging behind it three or four passenger cars. She felt the wind and she could see the running gear and the wheels of the locomotive spinning as it whooshed by her. She could see into the brightly lit passenger cars and could see people doing what people do on trains—some were sitting looking out the window, a group of men were playing cards, people in the dining car were eating. The only problem was they were not solid; Sarah could see through them as if they were only shadows. As the last car passed her, the rush of air blew out the flare and left her in total darkness. She turned in time to see the tail markers of the train reach Mosquito Creek, where they abruptly disappeared.

Silence now returned to the area. Sarah stared down the trail in utter disbelief at what just happened. Suddenly she was startled by her dad pulling up on his snowmobile.

"Where's your flare?" he asked. "I almost missed you!"

At first Sarah couldn't speak, and, dumbfounded, she simply pointed down the trail in the direction the train had disappeared.

Dad just looked at her, with a half smile on his face.

"Something wrong?" he asked

Finally Sarah found her voice. "Train! Train! A train just went by!!" she exclaimed excitedly. "I saw the steam engine and the cars and the people and I felt the wind as it rushed passed!"

Dad looked up as he filled the gas tank on Sarah's snowmobile. "There has not been a train through here in twenty-five years and there has not been a steam engine through here in sixty years. I think you fell asleep and were having a dream."

No matter how convincing Sarah was, Dad would not believe her. They got the sled running and headed home.

The next day Sarah got up early and went next door to her uncle and aunt's house. Her Uncle Chuck collected railroad stuff and was a bit of a local railroad historian. They sat in front of the fireplace in the living room and Uncle Chuck listened silently to her story, nodding occasionally in understanding. When Sarah was finished he got up and went into his study, returning a few moments later with a book. He flipped through a few pages and then handed it open to Sarah. "This might help you," he said.

Sarah looked at the open book. "Chapter Five: The Wreck of the 400," the top of the page said. Sarah took the book home and read how in the winter of 1933, a train wrecked at Mosquito Creek due to a siding switch being frozen open. The train was carrying passengers on their way to Eagle River. Seems a section boss was sent out in a "track car," which is basically a car that has train trucks on it and can ride on the rails. His job was to inspect the bridge at Mosquito Creek. He parked on the siding and during his inspection he heard the 400 coming and realized that he had forgotten to close the siding. He ran to the switch but by this time it had become frozen open. He couldn't get it closed. He tried signaling the engineer with a lantern but it was too late. The train was traveling at about seventy miles per hour and it derailed when it hit the open switch. Few survived the cataclysmic wreck. The book also contained a brief story on how people on or near the anniversary date of the wreck would see the train roar by, only to disappear at Mosquito Creek.

Sarah closed the book; she was going back to the trail the next night because that was the exact anniversary of the wreck. The next day, Sarah talked her sister, Maggie, and her three cousins, Doug, Charlie and Billy, to go back with her. She explained in detail the story she had read and what she had seen the night before.

The next night after dinner Sarah and Maggie got on the snowmobile and met their cousins at the end of the driveway. Doug and Billy were on one snowmobile and Charlie was on another. It was starting to snow as they headed south out of town to the bridge at Mosquito Creek. The sun had all ready set by the time they got there. Parking the snowmobiles along the old siding, they began to wait. After a few minutes they all started to get bored and began having a snowball fight. Suddenly the mayhem of the kids playing in the snow was abruptly interrupted by the long mournful distant sound of a steam whistle. The kids all recognized it instantly.

"It's coming," Sarah said in an astonished tone, as if she herself doubted what she had seen a few nights before. They all ran to the siding and watched as the train's headlight appeared down the trail. They could all feel themselves getting nervous. Billy, who was the youngest, hid behind his older brother Doug.

"I'm scared," he said in a quivering voice. Then something occurred that they were not expecting. A shadowy figure ran by them frantically waving a lantern.

"It's the ghost of the section boss!" Maggie shouted. By this time the kids were almost paralyzed with fear. They watched from a few yards away as the ghost of the section boss struggled in vain with the frozen switch. By some oversight when the tracks were removed years ago this switch was overlooked and remained.

"We gotta help him!" Doug shouted above the roar of the approaching train.

"Do what?" Charlie shouted in disbelief.

Doug ran over to the switch and began pulling on the control handle as hard as he could, and the rest of kids joined in, but even with their combined strength they could not budge it. The train was almost upon them and they were about to give up when seemingly out of nowhere, Dad and Uncle Chuck appeared out of the darkness. Dad had a long hollow pipe which he slid over the switch handle. He and Uncle Chuck pushed on it with all their might, and the kids joined in. Seconds before the train hit the switch, it let go and moved into the closed position. Everyone held on tightly as the ghostly train rushed by within inches of them. When the last car passed, they all turned to watch it cross Mosquito Creek. This time the tail lights did not suddenly disappear; instead they continued on down the trail towards Eagle River. Everyone watched until they were out of sight.

"How did you know we were here?" Sarah asked Dad.

"Uncle Chuck told me," he replied.

As they were turning to leave they were suddenly confronted by the ghost of the section boss. He stood there smiling at them, as if he had just been relieved of a huge burden. In his out stretched hand he held his lantern; he handed it to Uncle Chuck and then the old boss faded away. Uncle Chuck handed the lantern to Sarah.

"This is meant for you," he said.

The story does not quite end there; the people along the trail that night were treated to the ghostly specter of the 400 as it raced towards Eagle River one last time. When it reached town it stopped at the old station and townsfolk watched in disbelief as the shadowy passengers disembarked and faded from view as soon as they touched the platform, their long journey now complete. After all the people had gotten off, the train blew its whistle one last time, and as it began to chug out of the old station, it too faded from sight.

The townspeople don't know if the train will reappear along the trail next year, but they do know if it does, it won't be stopping at Mosquito Creek.

Dawn

"And the sea will grant each man new hope." I found myself mulling over this quote from Christopher Columbus as I watched the sun come up over the Atlantic Ocean. Dawn, a new beginning, and for me a sign that my world was once again about to change.

It was early fall 1945, and I had just been discharged from the hospital after spending the last seven months recuperating from injuries sustained when my ship—a fully loaded oil tanker—was sunk by a German U-boat in the north Atlantic. At that time the war was drawing to a close, and the sinking of my merchant vessel was one of the last of the war.

I remembered that day clearly. It had also begun with a sunrise over the Atlantic. Serving as third-shift watch officer I was the first to see the dawn as it broke over the deep blue ocean. I was also the first to see the track of the torpedo as it headed for the ship with its deadly, highly explosive cargo.

Strangely enough, it was dawn the next morning when, exhausted and burned, I was the last survivor pulled from the water by a Navy escort ship. I would spend the next seven months recuperating. Since the war was over by this time, the Merchant Marines had no place for me. So I was given my back-pay and my release papers along with a set of clothes and a new, dark blue pea coat. The next morning before the sun rose, I was released from the hospital and for reasons I cannot explain, made my way down to the ocean.

As the sun crept higher in the sky I could see that I was alone on the rocky New England shore. As if issuing a warning of the winter yet to come, a chilly ocean breeze caught me off guard and jolted me back to reality. Flipping up the collar of my pea coat I grabbed my seabag, which contained all my worldly belongings, and made my way to a nearby wharf on which rested a small café. Stepping inside the almost vacant diner I slid my bag into one side of a booth and sat on the other so I could look out onto the sea that had been my home for the last six years. Six years—had I been at sea that long? It did not seem possible, nor did it seem conceivable how much the world had changed in that time.

In 1939 I was a restless young man living in Marquette, Michigan. High school was behind me then and I had no prospect for a decent job or further education. The only work I could find was on the docks as a longshoreman. This was meaningless back-breaking work and not for a kid like me that longed for real adventure. So when I saw a chance to join the Merchant Marines out of Marquette, I took it. Little did I know then just what I had gotten myself into.

In 1939 war clouds were brewing over Europe. France had surrendered to the Germans and now they were pounding on the door of Great Britain. As a Merchant Marine I became a small link in the lifeline chain that helped Britain survive. Strange, isn't it? Suddenly a kid from northern Michigan, who had never even set foot out of the Upper Peninsula and had no plans for the future, was helping a nation on the far side of the world survive, and at the same time was helping defeat those who wished to impose their oppressive will upon the world. Thinking back, I guess my story is nothing new. Most of the young men and women that stepped forward to help defeat the greatest threat that civilized man had ever seen were similar in many ways to me. During my time with the Merchant Marines I had crossed the Atlantic dozens of times. On my very first trip we were hit by a torpedo near Ireland but managed to stay afloat and limp into port at Shannon. Our ship was beyond repair and most of the crew including myself was reassigned to a tanker, which I stayed with until it was sunk on that cold April morning.

Many sailors had come and gone in those six years but one person sticks in my memory. Floyd Lange. Floyd was one of the ship's engine mechanics. His knowledge of those big sixteen-cylinder monsters that drove us through the waves was uncanny. Simply put, he was the best mechanic in the fleet and by rights he should have been the chief mechanic, but he had problems with the bottle. At sea where there was no liquor to be found, he was safe. And he kept us all safe by keeping the engines running even in the most adverse conditions. Floyd is the guy that managed to get us into Shannon, Ireland, with one engine-room flooded and a gaping hole in our side. Even the captain was ready to abandon ship that time.

Once on shore, however, Floyd could not resist the siren call of alcohol. The captain would assign crew members to babysit Floyd whenever we were in port to ensure he stayed reasonably sober and got back to the ship by the time we sailed. I suppose the captain could have had him thrown out of the Merchant Marines but he knew he would never find anyone half as good. I, not much of a drinker, was often given the task of keeping an eye on him.

Despite our differences, we became good friends. No one knew a lot about him but I got some insight as we sat in the pub while on shore leave. After a few drinks he would start talking. He knew he was an appalling drunk and he knew that the only place he was safe was onboard ship. "That bucket of rust is my home," he would say in a melancholy tone, with speech slurred by the effects of the booze.

He also confided in me that he had a younger sister back home in Indiana and that every month his entire check was sent straight to her. "Deedee," he called her. I wondered how he got the money to pay for booze but that answer came when I discovered that he was quite a card player and rarely lost to anyone who was willing to take the chance to gamble with him.

Just before dawn on the morning we were torpedoed he had just come up to the bridge with a leather satchel about the size of an envelope. "You're the only person I trust," he told me. "Can you take these documents to my sister Deedee? She lives in Vermillion County, Indiana."

I looked at him quizzically.

"They are the documents she will need to claim my life insurance policy."

"What in the world are you talking about?" I asked, certain that Floyd had lost his mind or perhaps he was having some alcoholic relapse.

"This ship is the only place on this earth that I feel at home; it is the only place I can stay sober and be productive," he explained. "I owe this to my sister Deedee. Back home I was constantly in trouble with the law, drinking, gambling, running moonshine, you name it. If it was alcohol-fueled trouble, I was in it. My dad had the same problem; he ended up getting killed in an accident because of his drinking. Mom died several years later. Deedee was a lot younger than me but she took care of me and did her best to keep me out of trouble. One Sunday she returned from church to find me passed out on the back porch of the house. She poured a bucket of cold water on me and began to slap me in the face. When I sobered up she told me the Klan had come looking for me at church that morning. They were going to teach me a lesson for being a drunk. Truth of the matter was I got drunk the night before and drove a car right through the middle of one of their rallies. I splattered mud all over their imperial pooh-bah or whatever they call him."

Floyd smirked at me at this point. "Never much cared for those folk anyhow." He added, "Well it was painfully clear that the Klan intended to lynch me, so that night, Deedee, who was only fifteen at the time and didn't even have a license, drove me up to Detroit where my uncle was a Merchant Marine. He got me job on a ship bound for the Atlantic and I have been here ever since. It's been almost ten years since I last saw Deedee or any part of the United States except waterfront taverns."

"Why don't you mail these to her when we get to port?" I asked as I scanned the horizon with binoculars. Just then as the sun peeked over the horizon I spotted the wake of the incoming torpedo.

Before I had a chance to sound the alarm I heard Floyd say almost in a whisper, "Because I won't be going back to port."

I rang the collision alarm and ordered the helm to make a rapid turn, but it was too late. Within moments the ship was rocked by a terrific explosion on the starboard beam and began to list almost immediately as tons of water flooded into the barn-size hole created by the torpedo. The helmsman and I were thrown to the steel deck. Picking myself up, I realized that Floyd was gone. I looked out the door of the pilothouse just in time to see him as he entered the gangway leading below. The captain came into the pilothouse and ordered an immediate abandon ship; everyone knew she was destined for the bottom of the Atlantic. I secured the bridge as I was taught to do and was taking one last look around before I left when my eyes fell upon the leather satchel containing the documents Floyd asked me to take to his sister. I grabbed them and stuffed them into my shirt. Heading for the main deck I saw many of my crewmates come piling out of the crew quarters. Floyd was waking everyone up and sending them to the top deck. By now the ship was listing so much it became impossible to launch the lifeboats properly, so we cut several loose and let them fall into the water. Men jumped overboard and began climbing into them even though most of them were swamped or damaged from the fall. Moments later Floyd came out of the hatchway followed by choking black smoke and flame. I shouted his name. He briskly walked over to me, but I could tell by the look on his face he was focused on a single task. Without a word he grabbed a life vest and hustled me to the rail. I knew he intended to stay with the ship.

"Come on, Floyd, let's get off this tub," I said.

He pushed me overboard. "This is my home," I heard him say as he threw me the life jacket. "Now get the hell away from my ship."

I swam away hard and fast through the burning, oily water, and when I was far enough away I turned to see Floyd standing on the wing of the pilothouse. He could barely hold his footing as the ship listed. Suddenly cold water hit the boilers and the ship erupted in a horrifying explosion. This was followed by a second explosion as the 100,000 gallons of oil we were carrying ignited. Floyd was killed instantly. A moment later the ship was gone, leaving only a burning oil slick to temporarily mark its grave. I was not able to swim back to the swamped lifeboats. The current had separated us and my arms were burnt. I did manage to put on the life jacket Floyd had thrown me after he pushed me overboard and in it I floated for about the next twenty-four hours before being rescued.

Now, seven months later, as I sat in this diner I knew what I had to do. Reaching into my seabag I pulled out the oil-stained satchel Floyd had given me. A quick check of the documents to see if they were still legible and then I stuffed it back into my seabag. I had no idea if a place called "Vermillion County" existed and even it so, did this mysterious Deedee exist? All this could have just been the overactive imagination of man who partook in far too much alcohol, but that man was my friend so I figured I owed it to him to at least try to fulfill his final wishes. Paying for my breakfast, I asked the waitress the quickest way to the rail yards. Exiting the little diner on the wharf, I stopped to take one last look at the Atlantic, suspecting it would be a long time, if I ever saw her again. At the train station I was told that with all the westbound traffic of sailors and soldiers returning from the war that there were no seats available "for weeks." Acting on a hunch,

I waited until nightfall and then made my way into the rail yards. Sure enough, I found some hobos that gladly pointed out a freight train headed west.

Before I reached the train yard, I took off my new pea coat and stuffed it into my seabag. I then went to a second-hand store and bought a used coat. I needed to look as pathetic as the rest of them to avoid any unwanted attention. The darkness of the rail yard also helped. Hopping aboard a westbound freight, I soon found myself on my way. It's funny how different the world looks as you're zooming by at eighty miles per hour, even in the dark of night. Thanks to a full moon, I was able to see with relative clarity.

At dawn the following morning the train reached the rail yards in Roanoke, where I found a bite to eat at a local diner. After that I poked around the city for a while, then about dusk returned to the rail yards. Finding a bevy of bums, I sat with them near a fire and watched as they cooked some fish they had caught in a local stream. They kindly offered their meager meal but I declined. It was several hours before the train I planned to catch was due to depart, so foolishly, I opted for a nap. After an hour or so I was awakened by one of the hobos. He told me someone had grabbed my seabag and was running to catch a train that was leaving. I ran after slightly built man that, even though he had a head start, was so agile and fleet that he would have outrun me without that head start. He laughed at me as he ran. Then I saw him grab a handrail and try to swing himself up onto a moving boxcar. This is where his plan failed—the bum slipped and my bag fell to the ground. Losing his grip, he fell between the moving cars, where his legs were severed. Several of the other guys heard him screaming and gathered around but there was nothing we could do. In a moment he was gone. I grabbed my bag, and as an afterthought asked if anyone knew his name. Someone did, so I scribbled it on a piece of paper and pinned it to him. At least he would not die nameless. I didn't do this for him, for I held no sympathy for the petty thief.

I did it for those family members he may have left behind in case one day they came looking for him.

A few minutes later I boarded a westbound freight, this time on the Nickel Plate Railroad. This took me all the way to the town of Frankfort in Clinton County, Indiana. It is here one of the traffic clerks who worked in an office near the roundhouse shared his lunch with me and gave me instructions on how to get to Vermillion County, more specifically a small town called Dana, where I hoped to find Floyd's sister and give her the documents he wished her to have.

Hitching a ride on a flatbed truck, I soon found my way to Indianapolis, where the driver was kind enough to drop me off along the rail line of the Baltimore and Ohio. I started out on foot but soon was able to grab a ride on a passing freight. In an hour or two at right about dusk the freight reached a small town that seemed to appear out of the middle of a corn field. An old wooden sign post along the tracks identified it as Dana. I stepped off of the box car as it crossed Maple Street and made my way to a small diner about a block up. Taking a place in a booth I ordered a sandwich and a cup of coffee. When the waitress, a pretty girl about twenty-five with long dark hair and a smile, brought them, I asked her, "Do you know where I could find Deedee Lange?" Suddenly her smile disappeared and was replaced by a look of shock. "Floyd sent you," she said almost in a gasp.

I had traveled over 900 miles, most of it by boxcar, and not only found the small town I had never heard of but by sheer coincidence the first person I spoke to in Dana happened to be the one person I was sent to find. It's hard to explain the elation one feels at such a moment when you realize your journey wasn't for naught.

To say I was surprised by her response would be an understatement; I fumbled in my seabag and pulled out the leather envelope Floyd had given me on board our doomed vessel so many months ago. Still overwhelmed with sheer joy that I had accomplished Floyd's final wishes, I handed it to Deedee.

"What is this?" she asked.

"It's the forms to claim his life insurance policy. He gave them to me on the day he was killed and asked that I take them to you."

Deedee wiped away a tear and gently took the envelope from my hand. "I got the telegram from the War Department telling me he was missing and presumed dead, but they never explained how or why."

I asked if we could go somewhere and talk and she told me her shift was just ending and asked if I could come home with her. I finished my sandwich and coffee, grabbed my seabag, and we left the diner and walked to her home on nearby Briarwood Avenue, a small house with green shutters that backed up to the railroad line.

Along the way she told me that after the war started she took a job in a nearby munitions factory and worked there until just recently when she was no longer needed after VJ day. She also told me about her father and how he, like Floyd, had had a drinking problem and how he was killed when he fell from a box car almost directly behind the house. "He was drunk when he fell but the B&O railroad paid for his funeral, anyway. Mom buried him over at Bono Cemetery, and Floyd and I buried Mom there ten years later when she died."

We sat on the pack porch, our only light being cast from a railroad lantern with a cracked globe. She explained that it was the only memento she had of her father. "He was holding it when he fell," she explained. "I found it in the tall grass after they took his body away."

I began to tell her everything I knew from when I first met Floyd until the day we were sunk in the Atlantic and about my journey across the country to find her to fulfill her brother's last wishes. We continued talking until long after midnight and I never tired of her company. I tried to think of a reason to stay in Dana but there really was none, other than I liked this girl and it felt like I had known her my whole life. But one really can't say that to person you just met, can you?

Along about five thirty in the morning I heard the whistle of the train coming from the south. I told Deedee I had to go even though it was against every instinct I was feeling at that moment. She nodded and gave me a hug and before I could say anything she disappeared into the back door of her house. Not wanting to make a fool out of myself I grabbed my seabag and headed for the tracks. About ten minutes later the train chugged past me and I found an empty boxcar and climbed on board. Much to my surprise the train stopped and then backed up to do some switching at the grain elevator. After about fifteen minutes, with its switching task done, the engineer opened up the throttle and we began to head north. The first rays of sun were just starting to creep over the horizon and the train had just crossed Maple Street when I saw a dark figure come out from between the houses and make a dash for the train, more specifically the box car I was in. As he got close to the train he flung a suitcase into the box car. I reached out and grabbed the outstretched hand of the dark figure and pulled him on board.

"You made it," I said with a smile. To my incredible surprise the dark figure stood up and smiled back at me. It was Deedee.

"You never asked me how I knew Floyd had sent you," she said. "You see, nobody called me Deedee except Floyd. It was his nickname for me. It's actually my initials." She paused for a moment and just as the sun peeked over the fields of Indiana, she said, "My real name is Dawn."

More than five decades have passed since that day in Indiana. I, of course, married Dawn and we had four children and now have eight grandchildren. I wouldn't trade a day I've spent with her for anything. We return to Dana every so often. Her house is long gone and the train does not visit as often as it once did, but the town is basically the same. We have an old black and white picture of her parents from a happier time and a picture of Floyd and me when we were in the Merchant Marines that sits on our fireplace mantel. The only other memento she has is her father's railroad lantern with the cracked globe; it hangs in our kitchen greeting visitors as they come in the back door.

Christmas 1942

As every good historian knows, December 7, 1941, was a very important day in American history. It was this day that everything changed for the United States; it was the day that we were attacked by another nation and plunged into a conflict that engulfed the entire planet and touched almost every single family on Earth. Having been a child that grew up during the Depression and familiar with the concept of having to work and fight just to survive, I was more than willing to step forward to defend my country and my home as my father had done before me in the trenches of France in World War I.

So on December the eighth, even though I was only seventeen, I went down to the Navy recruiting office here in Frankfort, Indiana, to enlist, fully intending to do my part. When I got to the office I was told to go home and wait for my draft notice. Sorta like a "don't call us, we'll call you" kinda thing. Almost a year later I got that notice, but in the interim I did not sit around. I finished high school and was preparing to go to college when I got called up. Before I knew what was happening, and just days before Thanksgiving, I found myself on a train on the way to the Great Lakes Naval Training Center near Chicago, Illinois. To say I was a bit nervous entering this entirely unfamiliar, new world would be an understatement. Now, military basic training is a combination of physical fitness and testing to see what you're good at and polishing old skills like making your bed and cleaning up after yourself. After six weeks of this, the Navy decided I would make a good radio operator, so I was assigned to go to radio school down south.

But before I needed to show up there, I was given a pass, which is military talk for a short vacation. It was late on Christmas Eve 1942, and the only thing I could think of was going home to Frankfort to celebrate Christmas with my mom and dad. Now you have to remember that these were the days before airline service and super highways like you have today. Basically, my only choice was to try and hitchhike to Frankfort, which was unlikely, because it's cold in Indiana in December and it was snowing. Or, I could take the train, if I could find one.

Now, Chicago is the railroad capital of the world and had plenty of passenger trains departing everyday for places all around the country. I foolishly assumed that I could easily find a seat to Frankfort. So with my "pass" in hand I made my way to Union Station in Chicago only to learn that there was one seat available on the last train headed towards, but not stopping in, Frankfort. Having no other options, I bought a ticket on the Chicago, Indianapolis and Louisville, better known as the "Monon." I was the last to board and luckily found a window seat.

Storing my seabag, which contained all my worldly possessions, in the overhead compartment, I sat down as the train pulled out of the station and began its trip south towards Indianapolis. In a few minutes the conductor entered the car and began to collect tickets from the passengers. When he got to me I explained that I had just gotten out of basic training and was trying to get home for one last Christmas before I was sent overseas. The conductor never looked at me and continued to punch passenger tickets as he listened sympathetically to my story and my plea that the train make a stop in Frankfort, but he shook his head. "Sorry, son," he said without looking up. "We can't."

Heartbroken, I sat back down as the conductor exited the car. I looked out the window and tried not to think about how close I was going to get to home and not make it. I closed my eyes and I could see Mom at the big cast iron stove, cooking her usual

Christmas fare of snickerdoodles and other goodies, and a chicken for Christmas dinner. We always had chicken because Dad wasn't a big fan of turkey for some reason. And I could see Dad sitting in his favorite chair by the fire listening to the radio.

Heaving a deep sigh for what might have been, I opened my eyes and noticed that it had stopped snowing and stars were visible through the broken cloud cover. A full moon also shone down, lighting up the endless snow-covered Indiana fields. It was here I noticed that we were passing over the enormous trestle outside of Delphi, Indiana, and this I knew was only about twenty-five miles outside of Frankfort. I watched in vain as scenes familiar to me passed just outside my window. Wildcat Creek where I liked to fish, the small city of Rossville where my Dad and I stopped once to eat at a little place called The Sanitary Lunch, and finally the outskirts of Frankfort came into view. The clouds had moved back in and snow once again began to fall. Closing my eyes not to see my home town pass, I was suddenly shaken by the conductor.

"Grab your bag and come with me, son," he said. The conductor did not wait to see if I would follow, for he continued out the back of the train car. Quickly grabbing my seabag, I obediently followed him through the next car and out onto the vestibule. It was at this point I noticed the train had slowed significantly.

"I thought you told me that the train couldn't stop in Frankfort," I said.

With a hint of a twinkle in the old conductor's eye, he replied, "Who says we're stopping?"

Main Street Frankfort came into view and I simply stepped off the platform and directly onto the sidewalk as the train, slowed now to almost a crawl, continued on by. I was blocks from home. What had been impossible just moments before had become a reality. The sound of the steam engine adding power at the far end of the train brought me back to the moment. I looked up to say thanks to the conductor, and for the first time I noticed that he was a heavy-set man with red cheeks and a flowing white beard.

"Merry Christmas, son," he called to me, and I could hear his deep laugh as the train disappeared into the swirling snow. I watched in disbelief until the red Armspear marker lamps on the last car faded into the darkness. I looked down the street towards home, the lights on Christmas trees from the windows of several houses spilling out onto sidewalk. And suddenly it struck me as I stood there on that silent street with snow gently falling, just because the whole world seemed to be in turmoil and the future shrouded in uncertainty didn't mean that there was not magic left to be found at Christmas.

Lakota

It was the predawn hour of a new day. Dim light from the moon and stars cast eerie shadows upon the northern shore of Dollar Lake. For the fifth time in as many nights young Katherine had been awakened by an unfamiliar sound outside her bedroom window. She got out of bed and tried to rouse her sister, Robin.

"Robin," Katherine hissed silently. "I hear that noise again."

Robin, not being one to appreciate being awakened at such an early hour, grumbled, "Go back to sleep. You're having a dream."

And with that Robin rolled over and pulled the blankets over her head. Katherine, undaunted, went to the dresser and lit a candle in hopes that it would help her see into the darkness and find what was disturbing her night after night. She crept to the window, which was closed to keep out the early summer chill. Katherine held the candle up and peered out into the darkness. She could see nothing. Suddenly the hot wax from the candle dripped on her hand, and she inhaled sharply and looked down at her hand, shaking the hot wax off at the same time. While trying to desperately to get the burning liquid off her hand she unexpectedly heard the noise again outside the window. She looked up and there in the window, inches from her face, was the bloody face of a young man brandishing a tomahawk. Katherine screamed. Nathan, her dad, hearing his daughter's blood-curdling scream, leapt from his bed and ran into the girls' bedroom. Even in the pale moonlight Nathan could see Katherine, who was now pressed against the opposite wall of the room from the window, was as white as a ghost.

"WHAT IS IT!!??" Nathan shouted.

Katherine raised a trembling hand and pointed to the window. "There's a Indian boy out there," she stammered. "And he is covered in blood!"

Nathan ran for cabin door, passing Molly, his wife, who was also awakened by Katherine's scream, pausing only to grab his shotgun and lantern as he headed outside. Molly went into the girls' room and quickly retrieved the still-burning candle from the floor. She then went to Katherine, who was now huddled on the floor, shaking almost uncontrollably.

"What is it, Katherine?" Molly asked as she wrapped her arms around her daughter.

"Mom," she said, her voice quivering. "I heard a noise and when I looked out the window there was an Indian boy looking in at me and he was covered in blood."

From across the room came the voice of Robin, muffled by the blankets that were stilled pulled over her head. "YOU'RE HAVING A NIGHTMARE! NOW GO TO SLEEP!"

In a few minutes' time Katherine had calmed down, and a short while later Nathan returned from outside.

"There is nothing out there," Nathan said.

"Told ya," came the still-sleepy voice of Robin from underneath her blankets.

Nathan returned to bed and Molly made sure Katherine was going to be okay. Molly pulled the curtains closed on the window and as she left the room she heard Robin's muffled voice grumble, "If she would stop reading those scary books she wouldn't have this problem."

The sun rose early the next morning and quickly erased the dew from the landscape. Molly was in the kitchen preparing breakfast and Nathan was at the table tying pieces of fur onto a hook.

"What's that awful smell?" Molly asked.

"Skunk," Nathan replied. "I ran into Musky Todd yesterday in Eagle River when I took some pelts in and he said that muskie couldn't resist a lure tied with skunk fur. So I thought I would give it a try."

"Not so sure I would want to eat anything that ate skunk," Molly replied.

At that moment Katherine came in and sat down. "What's for breakfast?" she asked. "Skunk?"

Ignoring her question Nathan put his lure down and said, "Now tell us again what happened last night."

Katherine replied, "I heard that rustling noise again last night. It sounded just like it did before, like someone was dragging something down our path. I got up to look out the window and there was this Indian boy about fifteen years old standing there, holding a tomahawk like he was ready to strike. He looked like he had been badly beaten and there was blood all over him."

"Are you sure?" Molly asked from the kitchen.

"No doubt," Katherine replied.

She began to eat, and in a few minutes Robin came down the hall into the kitchen. She was wrapped in a blanket and her hair was a fright. She had just gotten up. Robin slumped down in a chair and in a sleepy voice commented, "It smells like Musky Todd in here."

After breakfast Katherine went out to look around the cabin for evidence to confirm what she had seen. She hunted around outside her bedroom window and could find no evidence that there had been someone there. Katherine searched for a good hour finding bits of beads, an arrowhead and other miscellaneous items that could have come from anyone and was just about to give up when she thought she spotted something sticking partially out from under a fallen log and concealed by some brush. She knelt down and carefully parted the grass. Much to her surprise, she found a doll made out of cornhusks that was caked in dirt and mud and looked like it had been there for time.

"MOM! DAD!" Katherine shouted. "Come here! I found something!"

Molly and Nathan came to investigate their daughter's findings. "Look, I found this doll," she stated.

Nathan picked up the doll. "I've seen these before," he said. "This was made by the Ojibwa." The Ojibwas were a tribe of Indians that still lived on the shores of nearby Catfish Lake.

"How can you tell?" Molly asked.

"They make these for the children during the fall harvest," Nathan replied.

"What's it doing here?" Katherine asked.

Nathan shook his head. Molly turned to go back into the house when suddenly she said, "LOOK!"

There, stuck in the house next to the bedroom window, was a tomahawk. Nathan jerked the tomahawk from the wall and examined it. It was covered in dried blood.

"Look as this!" Molly exclaimed. "It really is ornate and well made."

"Look, there is a carving of a wolf in the handle," Katherine added.

Nathan stared at the tomahawk and the doll and then said, "Let's go over to the Ojibwa village and see who they belong to. Maybe I'll bury it in the side of his home in the middle of the night."

After lunch, the family hiked around Dollar and soon found their way to the Indian village on the shores of Catfish Lake. Nathan knew the chief and asked permission to see him. After greetings were exchanged Nathan pulled out the tomahawk and the doll and showed them to the chief. The chief examined them with great interest.

"Where did you find these, Nathan?" he asked.

Nathan explained how the night before, Katherine had been awakened to find an Indian boy covered in blood staring in her bedroom window. And how when they searched outside of the cabin they found these items. The chief nodded his head then abruptly stood up and walked to the door of his teepee. He spoke native Ojibwa to someone outside for a moment then returned and sat back down. A few minutes later an old woman appeared. Without a word the chief handed this woman the weapon and the doll. The old Indian woman gasped.

"Lakota!" she exclaimed.

Nathan, Molly, Katherine and Robin looked at each other. "What's Lakota?" Molly asked in almost a whisper.

"It's Ojibwa for white girl who has nightmares," Robin replied sarcastically.

Molly silenced her with a glance. The old woman began to sob. "Lakota, Lakota," she said over and over again. She left the teepee sobbing and still clutching the items. The chief gestured that they should follow the old woman. Everyone got up and proceeded out of the tent. They followed her some distance from the camp to a small clearing; here there were what appeared to be three graves. The woman kneeled at one that was marked with round stone. In the stone was the carving of wolf. She clawed at the earth with her bare hands until she had dug down about a foot. In this opening she placed the tomahawk. Next she moved to a smaller grave where she buried the doll in the same manner.

After she was done she turned to the family and spoke in Ojibwa. The chief translated. "She says thank you."

"For what?" Nathan replied.

The chief explained, "Perhaps thirty years ago this woman was married and had two children, an older son who she called Lakota and a much younger daughter called Sooday. They lived here in the village and were very happy. One day it was Lakota's sixteenth birthday—in our village that is the time for a rite of passage. Lakota's mother and father presented him with a beautiful buckskin jacket and a knife and the tomahawk with the wolf carved in the handles because the name Lakota means 'wolf.' Since Lakota was now considered a man he assumed several new responsibilities, one of which was to watch over his little sister and always see to her safety. Lakota took this job very seriously. He loved his little sister, and she adored him. He swore no harm would ever come to her. One day Lakota and Sooday went to the village of Eagle River. Sooday loved to visit the trading post there because the proprietor would sneak her some candy every time she came in.

"Lakota and Sooday were headed back to the village after their visit to the trading post when suddenly they were attacked by a pack of wolves. The next day, everyone, including many people from Eagle River, went out to search for the brother and sister. The first thing found was the place the wolf pack attacked Lakota and Sooday. Nearby, four wolves lay dead, all from tomahawk and stab wounds. Also found were the remains of Lakota's buckskin jacket. A trail was picked up and followed almost a mile to the northern shore of Dollar Lake. Here they found Lakota; he had dragged himself after the wolves that had carried off Sooday. He was barely alive but managed to point down the trail and gasp out 'Sooday' before he died.

"The Ojibwa hunters continued following the blood-spattered trail a short distance until they found another dead wolf, this one with Lakota's knife buried in it, but no trace of Sooday's body was ever found. Lakota was carried back to the village and even today is regarded as a great warrior because no one had ever killed one wolf with his bare hands, let alone five.

"One day a year or so after this happened on a full moon night, the spirit of Lakota was seen near Dollar Lake. Just as you describe, covered in blood. Lakota's father knew that Lakota had come to find Sooday and bring her home. The father spent years looking for Sooday, knowing that was the only way his son Lakota would allow himself to rest. He never found the body either, and died searching for it." The chief paused. "Lakota is buried here, his father there," the chief said, indicating the graves. "The one marked there for Sooday is empty. Lakota refuses to allow himself any rest until Sooday is brought home."

After hearing the story the family returned home to their cabin on Dollar Lake. They remained silent all the way home and up to dinner that night before Molly spoke.

"Well, I guess you have your answer, Katherine."

Katherine said nothing but now knew what she had to do. That night a clear full moon was expected, and Katherine intended to help Lakota find his little sister. After midnight Katherine slipped out of bed, got dressed and left the cabin with a lantern to guide her. When she got outside she lit the lantern and was immediately startled to find Robin waiting for her.

"You didn't think you were going without me, did you?" Robin said.

Together the girls waited in the shadows of the towering pines. Soon they heard a familiar noise. The scrape of a person dragging himself down the trail. Katherine managed to suppress the urge to scream or cry out. She mustered all her nerve and managed to call out, "Lakota?"

The noise stopped just a few yards away from them. A shadow rose from the trail. In the dim light Robin and Katherine could see that it was indeed the spirit of Lakota. He gestured at Katherine and Robin to follow him and led them down the trail.

Katherine, who was closest, could clearly see that Lakota was badly injured. Deep wounds and bite marks covered his body and he limped, dragging an obviously broken leg. The sisters followed him for a good distance, when suddenly he stopped and pointed. They looked where he was gesturing and could see nothing in the darkness. Looking back at Lakota they saw him lie down then slowly disappear. Katherine and Robin began to search but could find nothing, even with the aid of the lantern. They marked the spot and returned home.

Early the next morning they returned to the spot. Their hound dog, Buster, tagged along.

"So what is it we are looking for?" Robin asked.

"A body," Katherine replied.

The girls hunted and hunted in the area indicated by the spirit of Lakota but could find nothing. Robin got bored and picked up a large stick.

"Come here, Buster," she said waving the stick at the hound. "Fetch," she said as she threw the stick as hard as she could.

The stick sailed through the air and hit the trunk of a big, dead oak tree. The girls were startled by the resounding hollow thump the tree gave off when the stick hit it. They headed for the tree. Katherine was the first one there and thumped on it with her fist. Turning to Robin she said, "It's hollow."

Picking up a large stone, Katherine beat on the trunk. She could feel the bark collapse under each blow. Suddenly the entire side of the tree gave way. Pieces of bark and sawdust rained down upon the girls. They stepped back and waited for the cloud to clear. When it did, they saw it. The body of Sooday was inside the hollow trunk. Somehow her being inside the trunk of the tree had preserved her body and she looked as if she had only been dead a short while.

The girls ran all the way to the Ojibwa village and found the old woman. She did not speak English so she could not understand what they were trying to tell her. Robin ran off and found the chief and dragged him by the hand to where Katherine was still trying to communicate with the old woman.

"Tell him," Robin said to Katherine.

"We found Sooday," Katherine explained to the chief.

Quickly they described how Lakota had returned the night before and led them to the spot and how the girls searched and found the body of little Sooday inside the trunk of the tree. The chief ordered several men to take the old woman and go with the girls. Soon they returned to the spot. The old woman recognized Sooday immediately and began to weep tears of joy, for she knew that Lakota would now be able to rest.

Sooday was carefully removed and placed on the ground while the men made a stretcher on which to bear the body home. While searching for materials to make this, one of the men found the bones of another wolf. This one's remains did not show wounds characteristic of a knife or a tomahawk. But oddly enough its neck had been broken. Then suddenly it had become clear to everyone. Lakota, as badly hurt as he was, had tracked and caught up with the two remaining wolves as they dragged the body of Sooday. With all his remaining strength he had killed one wolf with his weapons and then killed the last wolf with his bare hands. Lakota had found Sooday's body that day and hid her remains in the trunk to protect her until she was found. For he knew he was about to die and did not have the strength to carry her home. Lakota had not been looking for Sooday's body. He had been guarding it. Over time the tree had grown up and covered over her body, concealing it.

Sooday was carried back to the village and buried in the grave that had been waiting for her. That night the Ojibwas invited the family to a large feast in honor of Katherine and Robin. At dusk the girls slipped away to lay some flowers on the grave of Sooday. When they entered the clearing where the graves were, they were shocked to see several wolves lying on Lakota's grave. They backed up slowly, right into the Ojibwa chief, who had followed them.

"Do not be afraid. They will not harm you," the chief said. "It is a sign that the wolves respect him as a great warrior."

In a moment's time the wolves crept off into the waning light. Katherine and Robin laid a wreath of wild flowers upon Sooday's grave. As they were leaving the small clearing, Katherine turned around. There in the moonlight stood Lakota. He no longer looked battered and beaten, but clean and in a new buckskin jacket. Next to him, pulling on his hand, was the spirit of Sooday. Lakota looked at Katherine, and with his right hand pulled his tomahawk from his belt and held it horizontally over his head with the blade pointed away from Katherine. To Katherine's surprise the chief was still standing there and whispered to her, "He is saying you are his friend." Katherine held out her hand and waved. She could see Lakota smile as he and Sooday turned and disappeared into the shadows.

Sheamus

It was your typical fall Friday evening in Eagle River. The leaves had turned; most had fallen and could be seen racing down the side streets every time the cool wind blew. The sun was sneaking over the horizon a little earlier each day, people brave enough to face the late fall chill were out showing off their new fall jackets, and at Duffy's Tavern near the train depot, Sheamus (pronounced "Shaymus") McDuffy could be found tending his bar.

McDuffy had come to Eagle River in the early years of the twentieth century. He took over a failing establishment and made it profitable. He married a local girl, and together they raised five children. Sheamus was now long past retirement age and could have easily kicked back and enjoyed his twilight years. But ever since he took over the tavern five decades before he could be found working behind the bar, especially on a Friday night when the Chicago and Northwestern ran its "Sportsman's Special" for those who loved to come to Eagle River for the weekend to hunt and fish. Duffy's Tavern was the first place most of the passengers would stop, and McDuffy saw to it that they were always taken care of, and tonight would be no different.

The train arrived near its scheduled time and, as expected, a line of passengers made its way to the tavern, where they were greeted by a warm fire and cold drinks. It was about this time when Sheamus's youngest son, who was tending bar with him that night, pointed out the window. "Dad," he said, "look at that."

Sheamus looked out the window towards the station and could

see some young fellow slowly extracting himself from under one of the passenger cars.

"Hobo," Sheamus said. "He must have ridden the rods up here." Riding the rods was a very dangerous way to travel. It involved stretching boards under the car and riding there. To say it was dangerous would be an understatement; borderline suicidal, McDuffy called it. As they were watching, the conductor came along and spotted the man; as expected a chase ensued with the conductor waving a billy club as he ran after the freeloader. But fortunately for the hobo the conductor was old and fat and could not keep up.

McDuffy watched the chase as it angled towards his tavern and suddenly set down his tray of drinks on a nearby table and headed out the back door. He stood in the shadows, and when the bum ran by, McDuffy reached out and grabbed him and pulled him into the tavern, telling him to be quiet. A moment later the conductor came by, and McDuffy pointed down the hill towards the river. "He went that way," he said. "I think I heard a splash."

"Thanks," the conductor said, and ran down the hill.

McDuffy turned his attention back to the hobo. "Have a seat," he said as he ushered him into the bar.

"Thanks," the young man replied. He then added, "Why are you helping me?"

"Let's just say I've been where you are," McDuffy replied. "Would you care for a drink?"

"Ya know," the young man smiled, "I would really like a glass of Irish ale."

McDuffy poured him a glass and set it in front of him on the bar. The young man inhaled the aroma of the draft and grinned from ear to ear.

"AAAHHH," he said in pure satisfaction. "It seems like decades since I've had one of these."

McDuffy returned to his customers, and as the night wore on,

Sheamus's son went home early and the crowd began to dwindle, until only McDuffy and the young man remained.

"Where are you from?" McDuffy asked him as he cleaned up behind the bar.

"Chicago," the hobo replied.

"Getting kinda cold to head north, isn't it?" McDuffy asked. "Usually people are headed south this time of year."

"I've come to see an old friend," the hobo replied.

"Who?" McDuffy asked. "I know most everyone around here."

The hobo deflected the question by posing one of his own. "Who's that guy?" he asked, pointing at a picture behind the bar.

McDuffy turned to look to what the hobo was pointing at.

"That's James Morgan. He was a good friend of mine. He was killed in a train wreck in 1933 near Mosquito Creek."

"Oh, I remember that," the hobo replied. "Wasn't the engineer drunk and plowed into an open siding or something?"

McDuffy's mood turned suddenly icy towards the young man. "Morgan was the engineer. He was not drunk. He was one of the best men on the Chicago and Northwestern, and you're far too young to remember that."

"Looks like an idiot to me," the young man said with a slight twinkle in his eye, clearly trying to provoke McDuffy.

It worked. "You can say anything you want about me," McDuffy said. "Tell me my bar is a dump, say my drinks are terrible, tell me my dog is ugly, but don't you ever be insulting my friends."

"Calm down, old timer," the young man said. That tore it. McDuffy may have been old but he was not incapable of taking care of himself. With one burly hand he grabbed the young man from his seat and lifted him clean off the floor. Putting his face right up to the young man's, in a very quiet and stern voice he said, "You've worn out your welcome here, laddie, and it's time you leave."

The young man just smiled back at him, then started to chuckle.

"It's good to see you again, Sheamus," he said. In an instant McDuffy suddenly recognized him.

"Morgan!" McDuffy gasped, and at the same time he let him go. James Morgan ended up in a heap on the floor. Laughing, he picked himself up and dusted himself off.

"It can't be! You're dead! You died in that wreck in '33. I carried your coffin, and you're buried right over here in Eagle River Cemetery."

"All true," Morgan said with a grin.

"Why? . . . How?" was all McDuffy managed to say, which considering the fact that he was being confronted by his long-dead friend at that moment, made it impressive that he could get *that* out.

Morgan just grinned back at him, kinda shrugged and said, "It's been a long time, old friend."

After a few moments, McDuffy was able to compose himself, deciding that he was dreaming and that he would play along since he was obviously sleeping, anyhow. The two old friends began to talk about what old friends talk about. They rehashed old fishing and hunting trips: *Do you remember the white buck we saw at St. Germain? Remember the muskie that I caught with a cane pole? The time we fished through the ice on Kentuck Lake for walleyes? When we camped at Franklin, how quiet it was in the morning and that mist hung over the lake? Do you remember when you shot that quail and that grey fox came out of nowhere and stole it before it hit the ground? Do you remember the barn owls on Big Saint? And the hoot owl at Razorback?* They talked and laughed all night, and right about the time the first rays of sun started to peak on the eastern horizon, Morgan stood up and said, "Well, it's time to go, Sheamus."

McDuffy stood too and said, "Okay. In spite of this scare you have given me, it has been good to see you, James."

Morgan slowly shook his head. "You don't understand, Sheamus; it's time for you to go."

"Where am I going?" McDuffy asked.

Morgan tilted his head towards the fireplace, indicating McDuffy should look over there. McDuffy turned and looked to see someone sitting in a chair by the fire.

"Who's that?" McDuffy asked quietly.

"It's you, old friend. You've been dead most of the night."

"DEAD?" McDuffy said, his normally strong voice having a slight quiver. "I can't be dead! What about my bar? Who will run Duffy's Tavern? Who will be here to greet the passengers from the 400 on Fridays?"

"I suspect your sons will, and they'll make you proud."

"I can't go; I've got too much to do."

"Mary Ann is waiting for you," Morgan said.

The words brought McDuffy to a dead stop.

"Mary Ann?" he asked cautiously. Morgan nodded.

Mary Ann McDuffy was Sheamus's wife of over forty years. He first met her when he hired her to cook at Duffy's, and boy, could she cook. She made normal pub fare, like burgers, fried chicken and pizza, and also made the best perch, panfish and walleye around—all freshly caught, of course. In summer they had cook-outs and invited the entire town. Mary Ann cooked it all, and no one went away hungry or dissatisfied.

Well, they fell in love and had five children and spent forty-two years together as happy as can be. But Mary Ann had fallen ill several winters ago and died. Sheamus was so upset he could never bring himself to speak of her. When she died, McDuffy pulled the stove out of the tavern, hauled it down to the river and threw it in, stating that no finer meals than the ones Mary Ann cooked could ever come from that stove again, so clearly there was no point in keeping it.

After that, McDuffy's sons spent weeks trying to convince him to replace the stove and that serving warm food was key and one of the reasons Duffy's was so popular. But he would not discuss it, so his sons took it upon themselves and had a new stove was installed one Sunday night, and by Friday, with one of his son's wife now cooking, the kitchen was in full swing and ready for the Friday night crowd. McDuffy's way of acknowledging that his sons were right was to say nothing about it, and just took it in stride.

McDuffy sighed, took one long look at the body in the chair by fire, and then looked around his bar one last time. He nodded to himself in satisfaction.

"Let's go, James," he said. "By the way, how's the fishing where we're going?"

He turned to see Morgan standing behind him; in each of his hands he held a fishing pole, the same two poles Sheamus had kept above the bar since Morgan's death. In fact, they were Morgan's poles; his widow had dropped them off at Duffy's after James was killed.

"The fishing where we are going is absolutely the best," he replied, then paused. "But, it's not as good as Dollar Lake," he said, handing Sheamus one of the poles.

"Isn't Mary Ann waiting?" McDuffy asked.

"Yep, but she understands that you will be late," Morgan said with a grin.

As you may have already guessed, McDuffy was buried in Eagle River Cemetery, next to his beloved Mary Ann. His sons took over the tavern and ran it for many years until a fire forced them to close, about the same time they decided that the place wasn't the same without their dad. So they razed what was left of the tavern and then donated the land to city of Eagle River.

As for the two old friends, it is said that on a clear quiet morning, when the air is still and the lakes are as smooth as glass, you may see them in the early morning mist, fishing poles in hand, walking down the dirt road that leads to Dollar Lake.

Good Night, Tommy

Tommy Goodfield grew up on the shores of Pine Lake. Born in the last decade of the twentieth century, he got to experience many things even his parents didn't just a generation before. Computers, cell phones, and later on, Wi-Fi, iPods and iPads kept the world at his fingertips to a degree the generation before his could not imagine.

When Tommy was about two years old, his grandmother passed away. Worried about her father's well-being, Tommy's mom convinced her dad to move in with them on Pine Lake. Besides some basic personal items such as his clothes, the only thing that Tommy's grandfather owned was a 1957 Chevy Bel-Air convertible that he called "Mable." Granddad kept his classic car in pristine condition, washed her weekly, waxed her about four times a year and never drove Mable in the winter months when the caustic salt spread on the highways caused even modern cars to rot. Despite their difference in age, Tommy and his grandfather were almost constant companions as Tommy grew up. This was nice for Tommy for many reasons, but especially since his dad was a local attorney and worked long hours.

Granddad taught Tommy to fish, hunt, camp and respect the forest. And much to everyone's surprise, when Tommy turned sixteen, Granddad taught him to drive in his beloved Mable. Tommy, short in stature at the time, had to sit on a folded blanket to be high enough to see over the giant steering wheel. When Tommy was seventeen, Granddad even let Tommy take it on dates. The girls loved the old car and Tommy got a kick out of being the only kid in his school that could drive a three-speed manual transmission, "three on the tree," as it's more commonly known.

Now let me back up for a minute, because Granddad has a past to that you need to know about. Granddad lived most of his life in Vilas County. When he turned eighteen, he went to work for the county, driving garbage trucks and doing road maintenance, until he was about twenty and was drafted into the Army. He served four years, two as a military police officer and two in combat in some of the worst fighting of the Vietnam War.

When he left the Army, he returned to Vilas County and became a deputy sheriff. And by his own choice, he worked the late shift, partially because his high school sweetheart was the late shift dispatcher and partially because it was usually quiet on the late shift, so as he patrolled the Vilas County highways he was able to pick up the "Radio Mystery Theater" on the air on KMMQ out of Chicago on his squad car's radio. It was a throwback to the days when radio was the only form of media available. Most of the country had long turned off Radio Mystery Theater by this point in history, and KMMQ was one of the last to broadcast it. And since the station was AM, it was allowed to boost its power at night, which usually made the signal come in loud and clear, even in northern Wisconsin.

The shows were usually about a police detective and his dealings with criminals; most were an hour long or so but sometimes they would run over several nights, predictable with cheap sound effects and often with one or two people playing several different roles while trying to disguise their voices from the listening audience. It was campy at best, but Granddad liked it. Every night after the show was over, the radio station would sign off around three in the morning, with one broadcaster giving the station identification: "This is KMMQ Chicago signing off." Then the announcer would always add, "Say goodnight, Tommy," and whoever "Tommy" was would respond, "Goodnight, Tommy."

Granddad adopted this phrase in his work. Whenever he arrested someone he would handcuff them, and as he placed them in his squad, he always said, "Say goodnight, Tommy." Most of the people he dealt with didn't get it or, per the norm, were too intoxicated to understand. But he didn't care; to him it was funny.

Well, as you probably already guessed, Granddad married his high school sweetheart and they had one daughter. She grew up, got married and had a son whom she named "Tommy" in honor of her dad, which was a source of great pride for Granddad. And as you already know, Tommy spent a lot of time with his grandfather as he grew up.

Every time something significant happened to Tommy, Granddad would go out to visit his wife's grave at the Eagle River cemetery and tell her all about it. "Tommy lost his first tooth today," or "Tommy got an A on that math test he was worried about," or "Tommy caught a muskie today," or "You should see Tommy's new girlfriend—she is as pretty as you were at that age." But it wasn't just the good stuff he spoke to her grave about. One visit in particular stands out, when what he had to say so unnerved him he could barely raise his voice above a whisper. "Tommy joined the Army today." And that is all Granddad could say to the grave of his beloved wife that day.

Yes, this was a sore subject with Tommy's parents and his grandfather. Tommy's counter-argument was that his dad and grandfather both served in the Army, and he felt he should too, and he would not change his mind. The day came when Tommy had to leave. Granddad drove him to the airport in Rhinelander along with his parents and his girlfriend. When it became Tommy's turn to board the airplane, he turned to his grandfather and said, "I left you a present in Mable's glove box," and before Granddad could reply, Tommy was down the jet way and on board the aircraft. Returning to the car, Granddad found Tommy had left him a complete collection of CDs containing the old KMMQ broadcasts of Radio Mystery Theater. It brought Granddad to tears. The very next day Granddad had a CD player installed in his Bel-Air, the only upgrade he ever made to the car, so he could listen to the CDs.

Granddad also bought a laptop computer and learned how to use it; he did this so he could talk to Tommy through e-mail. Now Tommy's parents would talk to him through e-mail as well. But he never told them anything that might scare them or make them worry about him. He did, however, tell his grandfather things he thought might upset his parents. And Tommy's grandfather kept it to himself. Tommy went with his unit to Iraq and Afghanistan. He always told his parents that he was never in any danger but Granddad knew his unit was in the thick of the fighting. Every night he sat in Mable out in the driveway listening to the CDs Tommy left him and waiting for messages on his laptop. Sometimes Tommy's mom would find that he had sat in the driveway all night.

Finally after almost a year, Granddad got the e-mail he had been hoping for. Tommy was coming home; he had finished his tour and would be home in less than a week. He asked his grandfather not to tell anyone and requested he meet him at the airport in Rhinelander. Granddad said he would be there.

Five days later Tommy came out of the terminal in Rhinelander to find his grandfather in Mable waiting for him. It was a joyful reunion. They drove back to Eagle River together. All the way Tommy talked in detail of his experiences, some of them pretty grim, close calls, lost friends, things that happen in war. Granddad listened and nodded his head in understanding, commenting once in a while. What were a year ago a boy and his grandfather had now become two combat veterans. When Tommy asked how his grandfather dealt with the memories of what he had seen, he replied, "I find a lot of pleasure in the simple things. Like a good campfire on a brisk fall evening, or a good day fishing on a calm, secluded lake. It's stuff like that I missed the most while away, and

I learned things like that are gifts, and gifts come and go and aren't always forever, so we should never waste them."

When they got to Eagle River, instead of heading straight home, Granddad drove to the cemetery. "I've got to tell Grandma you're home," he said with a smile. "You take Mable and go home. Your folks will be glad to see you."

"I can wait, Granddad," Tommy replied.

"No, I've got a lot to tell Grandma tonight, and besides I really enjoy the walk."

With that Tommy took Mable and headed for home. He was about to pull in the long driveway that led to the house when, much to his surprise, Mable's engine died. Try as he might, he could not get her to start. So he walked the rest of the way up the driveway and strode into the house. His mom nearly went into shock, and Dad was equally as emotional. It was a tearful reunion, to say the least—questions asked, tears shed, stories told. Then when things initially calmed down, Mom told him. "There is some bad news." Tommy looked at her. "Granddad died three days ago."

Tommy's expression didn't change. "What's the joke?" he responded.

Mom got a little incensed. "No joke, Tommy, we buried him this morning, and to make matters worse, someone stole Mable out of the garage while we were gone."

Now Tommy became a little indignant. "I have Mable," he replied. "Granddad picked me up in Rhinelander a couple hours ago. I dropped him off to talk to Grandma . . ." Tommy's voice trailed off. He then got up and went out the door, and Mom and Dad followed. They walked down the driveway and found Mable on the road. Dad reached in and turned the key; the engine turned over then started without hesitation.

Without a word they all got in and Tommy drove them to the cemetery. They got out and walked to the plot that held Grandma's grave, and Tommy could clearly see that there was indeed a fresh grave next to his grandmother's. Clearly this was not a joke. Staring at the grave of his grandfather he explained how he had e-mailed him just about a week ago and ask him to pick him up in Rhinelander.

Somewhat stunned, they walked back to the car. When Tommy got in, he sat on something. It was his grandfather's favorite fishing lure in the box he always kept it in. He opened the glove compartment to put it in and a piece of paper fell out. It was the title to Mable and it was in Tommy's name. Too shocked at the recent events to say anything, he started the car, and when the engine came to life so did the CD player. Through the speakers they heard, "This is KMMQ Chicago signing off. Say goodnight, Tommy."

Then to everyone's surprise, what was clearly Granddad's voice came through the radio loud and clear. "Goodbye, Tommy."

Now, the story does not quite end there. The other day I was out early for a walk when I came across a sheriff arresting a drunk driver. As he placed the suspect into the back of his squad car I thought I heard the officer say, "Say goodnight, Tommy."

Grandpa's Rifle

When I was just a little guy, I used to come down here and visit my grandfather that lived on a farm here in Clinton County. He is gone now and this family farm was sold off decades ago, but I can still picture it as if it were yesterday. The farmhouse was made of stone and had a tremendous handmade brick fireplace, complete with an old Springfield rifled musket that hung above the hearth.

I asked my grandfather about that rifle once and he told me that it had belonged to his grandfather, who used it in the Civil War. Well, ya know I just couldn't leave that alone. I just had to ask, "Did he shoot any Rebels with it?" Granddad messed my hair. "Well," he explained, "My grandfather never spoke of the war, but there was a story my grandmother used to tell me, that he once saved an entire regiment of Rebel soldiers with it."

Granddad didn't wait for me to ask the details. He just lit his pipe and began to explain. "Seems it was at the end of the Civil War, when your Great-Great-Grandpa Jacob was just about twenty years old and he served in the 24th Indiana from Lafayette. They were down in eastern Tennessee, where they encountered a regiment of Rebel soldiers. Now you see, Robert E. Lee had surrendered the Confederate forces two weeks before and for all intents and purposes, the war was over. By this time this fact was widely known by both sides of the conflict. Unfortunately, this Confederate unit was led by a fanatical colonel who refused to recognize the surrender. The Union scouts reported that even though his men were vastly outnumbered, sick and starving, the Rebel colonel was planning an all-out attack against the battle-hardened 24th. Anyone could see it was going to be a meaningless slaughter of the already-defeated Rebel soldiers.

"It was at this point Grandpa Jacob took it upon himself to try and bring the situation to a close with as little loss of life as possible. He took that very rifle and climbed a small hill overlooking the battlefield. He could see the Rebel colonel through his field glasses; he judged the distance to be close to 300 yards, which is the maximum range of the Springfield rifled musket. He took a moment to gauge the wind and then, with one shot, he killed the Rebel colonel. With their fanatical leader now gone, the second in command quickly surrendered. Great-Great-Grandpa Jacob saved untold lives on both sides that day. After the war, he retuned to Indiana, bought some land and built this very farm. He then hung his rifle over the fireplace and swore that as long as he lived he would never kill another living thing. As long as I knew him," my grandfather explained, "he never did. When he died, decades later, a group of former Confederate soldiers came to pay their respects, and as a way of saying thanks they gave Grandmother their coveted regimental flag."

Well, I thought that story was pretty cool, but I kinda doubted it until one day when I was about twelve years old. I was out exploring on the farm. I had gotten a good distance from the house when suddenly I encountered a mountain lion. I had come to a small creek to throw rocks in when I saw the big cat drinking from the stream. Fortunately, I saw him first and that gave me a slight chance to get away. I ran for the house yelling for Granddad, and as I ran I saw him come out of the barn with the gun he kept there. I looked back to see the mountain lion clear the stream with one jump and come straight for me as fast as he could. Within seconds he covered the short distance between us, and as he leaped into the air to pounce on me I heard several gunshots. A bullet passed within an inch of my ear, struck the cat dead-center and flung it backwards with tremendous force. The animal landed with a thud several feet away and lay motionless. I knew it was dead, killed instantly by the bullet from my grandfather's gun. I stood there staring at the dead animal, trying to get a grasp on what just happened.

I think it was a good five minutes before Granddad came running up. "Granddad, you got him!" I said. "That was an incredible shot."

He looked at the dead cat and slowly shook his head. "It wasn't me. I was afraid I would hit you so I was firing in the air trying to scare it off."

There were other farm houses nearby so we assumed someone else must have shot the big cat. That is, until we got back to the farm house. Grandma was waiting on the porch. "I was upstairs and I heard all the commotion," she explained. "I looked out the window and I could see you being chased by the mountain lion. So I ran downstairs and was about halfway down when I heard the gun shots. I ran out on the porch and that was sitting there." At first I thought she was pointing at the old rocking chair, but then I did a double-take. There behind the rocker, leaning up against the house with smoke still drifting out of its barrel, was Great-Great-Grandpa Jacob's 1863 Springfield rifled musket.

"You shot the mountain lion?" I asked.

Grandma shook her head. "I've never fired a gun in my life," she said. I looked inside the house; sure enough, the rifle above the fireplace was missing. It seemed impossible but there was no other explanation. Clearly my great-great-grandfather Jacob had somehow once again used his rifle to save the life of the innocent.

Today I own my own farm in another state. The land is full of corn, where my children now play among the rows and I can stand on the porch and see over the fields to the spot near a creek very similar to where I encountered the mountain lion decades ago. My farm house is more modern, with the exception of the brick fireplace. I had it built as close as I could to the one that was on Great-Great-Grandpa Jacob's farm. As for his 1863 Springfield rifle, it hangs above in a place of honor, except now I make sure it's always clean and ready. Because I know Great-Great-Grandpa Jacob is always watching over us, and I want it ready should he ever need it again.

Gus

To some, "paradise" is the abode of the righteous, a place good people are sent when life is over. To others, paradise is much simpler: a circle of chairs filled with family and friends beneath the shade of a towering maple tree, or maybe the view awarded to those who choose to scale foothills or mountains. To Molly and Nathan, paradise was their new home on White Tail Lake. Towering pines swaying ever so slightly in the evening breeze, a lake as flat and calm as glass, the only sound the echoing cry of the loon.

Tonight was such a night. Nathan sat on the dock overlooking the lake, the sun was just setting, and blazing streaks of red and orange stretched across the sky. In a few moments Molly joined him, and they sat quietly discussing the day's events and what they might do tomorrow. The sound of footsteps alerted them to the presence of their two daughters, Katherine and Robin.

"What are you guys doing up?" Nathan asked them in a semi-stern voice.

"We can't sleep," Katherine replied sleepily.

"Why?" Molly asked.

"Because someone across the lake is playing a violin or something," Robin said.

Nathan and Molly had not noticed it before but when they turned to listen, sure enough, they heard it. Very soft and very precise, the notes floated across the lake. "I think that is Mozart," Molly said. Nathan nodded in agreement.

"What's Mozart?" Katherine asked.

"Not what, who," Molly explained. "Mozart was a composer."

They sat there and listened as the music faded away with the setting sun. Quiet then returned to the lake.

"Bed," was all Nathan needed to say, and without a word of protest, Katherine and Robin scurried back to the cabin. For the next several nights, right at sunset as Nathan and Molly sat on the dock, they could clearly hear the notes of various Mozart melodies drifting across the water. Finally, one morning the family got in the boat and headed off across the lake. After rowing a few minutes they approached the area that they thought they had heard the violin music coming from the nights before. All they could see from the water was a dock, old but in good condition. Nathan brought the boat in and tied it off as the girls and Molly stepped out. Together they walked up the path from the lake and found a tidy little cabin in a perfect storybook setting with green shutters surrounded by a flower garden and a neatly trimmed lawn on which sat a handmade picnic table. They looked around the house and yard a little bit when suddenly a voice with a heavy accent called out to them, "Can I help you folks?"

Nathan and Molly turned around to find an elderly man just a few feet behind them. Molly, having been caught off guard, stammered as she answered, "We're sorry! We didn't know anyone lived here. We didn't mean to trespass."

"It's okay," the stranger said. "It's good to have visitors. I am called Gus," he said, introducing himself.

"Are you the one playing the violin in the evening?" Nathan asked him.

"Why, yes," Gus said with a smile. "I play for my darling Anne."

"We live across the lake and heard your beautiful music; we just had to find out where it was coming from," Molly said.

"Who are these young ladies?" Gus asked, smiling at Katherine and Robin.

"These are our daughters," Molly replied, introducing them.

"Please, sit," Gus said, indicating a small circle of chairs around a pit where a low fire was burning. They sat down as Gus disappeared inside the cabin, returning a few minutes later with a pitcher of lemonade in one hand and a violin in the other. As he opened the door, a yellow and white cat came out with him.

"This is Tiger," he explained. "He is my best friend, next to Anne."

Tiger rubbed past Robin's legs, then jumped into Katherine's lap and settled right in. "He likes you," Gus said as he served the lemonade to his guests.

Next, he put down the pitcher and picked up the violin. "I usually only play for my Anne but she is not here right now," he explained. He then placed the instrument under his chin and for the next forty-five minutes or so played the most beautiful classical music they had ever heard. It was so moving that even Nathan had to wipe away an occasional tear. Finally, Gus stopped and set his violin on the table. Molly thanked him and said it was the most wonderful music she had ever heard. The family got up to leave, and as Gus bade them goodbye he said, "I am sorry Anne was not here to visit. She will be sorry she missed you."

With that, Nathan, Molly, Katherine and Robin got in their boat and headed back across the lake. As they rowed away, they could see Gus waving from his dock with Tiger sitting on the edge of the pier. That evening as they sat on their own dock at sunset they once again could hear Gus playing.

The next day while Molly and Nathan were clearing some brush they happened to see their neighbor.

"Hey, Jim!" Nathan called out.

Jim came over. "Afternoon, Nathan, afternoon, Molly," Jim said, tipping his hat.

"Did you hear that violin last night?" Nathan asked.

Jim shook his head. "No," he replied. "But some time ago old

Gustavo used to play Mozart in the evening for his wife, Anne. Usually could hear him right about sunset."

"Gustavo?" Molly asked.

Jim nodded and began to explain. "Gustavo was his real name but we all called him Gus. He and his wife, Anne, lived on the far side of the lake for years. They were here long before I moved here. Nice couple, but a little hard to understand. They came from Austria, I think. Immigrated to America back in the 1850s. They were one of the first people to build here on White Tail. Anne loved Mozart, and Gus, who was classically trained on the violin, would play for her every night." Jim paused to try and light his pipe, and then continued. "Anne died about five years ago. Poor Gus, I'd never seen a man so heartbroken. He was never the same, but he did stay here on the lake. We didn't see him much after that. Once in a while you would spot him fishing off his dock. A couple years ago he adopted a stray kitten he found lying near death in the woods. Nursed him back to health, and as far as I know, that cat was his only companion."

"Tiger," Molly said.

Jim once again paused and tried once more to light his stubborn pipe while giving a rather quizzical look to Molly. "How did you know he called his cat Tiger?" he asked.

Before she could reply Nathan asked, "Does he still play the violin every evening?"

"No," Jim replied shaking his head. "Gus died several months ago, just before you moved here. Ever since then it's been quiet in the evening. To tell you the truth, I kinda miss it."

Molly and Nathan stared at Jim, who didn't notice because he was still trying to light his pipe. Finally giving up, he turned it over and tapped it on the heel of his shoe to clean it out. "His place has been empty ever since," he explained further. Packing his pipe with fresh tobacco, Jim bid them good day and left.

Without a word, Nathan and Molly dropped what they were

doing and headed for the dock. In a few moments' time, they were pulling for the distant shore, and in a few minutes' time they reached Gus's dock and tied off the boat. Nathan was the first out and when he stepped down his foot went right through a rotted piece of board. As he extracted his now-soaking-wet foot he noticed that the entire pier appeared to be in disrepair. "This is worse than I remember," he said.

They headed up the little path, which was now strangely overgrown with weeds. When they reached the cabin it no longer looked pristine. Two of the shutters were hanging off at odd angles and a large tree limb was down across the roof. The chairs they had sat in just the day before were tipped over, and the neat yard was now well overgrown. Everything was in disarray from months of neglect. Nathan held his hand to the fire pit. "This is stone cold," he said. "There has not been a fire here in months, but that is impossible. Was it a dream?"

Molly reached down into the tall grass next to the now overturned picnic table and picked up the empty lemonade pitcher, now dusted inside and out with dirt and partially full of stagnant rain water.

"I don't think so," Molly replied, her voice noticeably shaken. Next, they went to the cabin and peered through the dirty windows. The only thing they could see was the violin Gus had played for them the day before sitting in an open case on the kitchen table. It was covered in a heavy layer of dust.

"Let's get out of here," Nathan said almost in a whisper. They quickly headed back down the overgrown path to the dock, and much to their surprise, found Tiger the calico cat sitting in their boat.

"Gus's best friend next to Anne," Molly said quietly.

Nathan tried to shoo Tiger away, but the cat gave no indication that he intended to leave the boat. Nathan was not about to argue, so they got in the boat and rowed for home. When they got back to their dock Tiger jumped out of the boat and ran to the house.

Katherine and Robin saw him and, smiling, asked in unison, "What's this?"

"Our new pet, I guess," Molly replied with a shrug.

That night as Nathan and Molly sat on the dock at sunset they again heard the faint strains of Mozart. Somehow they knew they would never again hear it played by him, for they now understood that it was Gus saying thank you for giving his best friend a new home, and it was also Gus saying goodbye.

Mrs. A and the Muskie

I was going through some long-neglected boxes in my office the other day and I discovered an old article I had tucked away some time ago about a woman in Vilas County who had landed a trophy muskie on her dock at Pine Lake. The picture that accompanied the photograph showed a spry woman in her seventies grinning from ear to ear, while a young man of about fifteen held up the oversized, elusive game fish for the newspaper photographer. The caption under the picture identified the woman as "Mrs. A." The young man in the photo was me. I grew up in a small house on the shore of Pine Lake, and as long as I could remember, Mrs. Anna Alexiconofski was our neighbor. You can see why she had the nickname of "Mrs. A."

Her modest two-bedroom, ranch-style, gray home sat on the north side of the lake on a rise; it was connected to the road by a long driveway that looped in front of a two-car garage. A small breezeway connected the garage to the house, and on the back of the house, a large letter "A" hung on the wall.

As long as anyone could remember, she lived alone. Mrs. A had many friends, though. She was a very happy person and was always curious about people and things. She was also a mystery—she had a very distinct accent and no one knew anything about her past. Even people who knew her well knew very little about who she was and where she had come from. She never got mad when friends pressed her for information about her past. She would politely say, "My past is not worth discussing." If pressed for an answer she would only shake her head and smile.

Growing up next door to her, I noticed that she often seemed to be watching down her driveway for someone or something. At night there was a single candle glowing in her kitchen window.

One time Mrs. A saved my life. It was deep wintertime, right about dusk. I was playing out on the ice. I broke through and couldn't get out. As I struggled, I saw Mrs. A come running down the hill from her house. Without a moment's hesitation she grabbed a long branch and, lying on the ice, held it out to me. To this day I remember that she was not wearing any winter coat, just a sweatshirt advertising her beloved Green Bay Packers. Within a minute she had me out of the freezing water and she half-carried me to my house where my parents, hearing the commotion, met us at the door. As I sat shivering in a blanket near the fireplace and as Mom scolded me for being out on the ice, I remember Mrs. A tussling my hair and saying with a smile, "This is nothing. Where I come from that lake is the same temperature as bath water."

Even though she lived on a lake, Mrs. A was not big on fishing. As far as I know she only had three regular hobbies, hiking in the woods, reading and listening to the Green Bay Packers on a small transistor radio. I used to see her sitting on her dock in a lawn chair, wearing store-bought magnifying glasses, reading a book. She did keep a fishing pole nearby with a line in the water, which until one day seemed strange to me. I was bored one summer afternoon, sitting on the back step of my house, whittling nothing particular on a stick I found nearby, when suddenly I heard her shout. I dropped what I was doing and ran for her dock.

When I got there I saw her lawn chair tipped over and the book she had been reading was floating in the lake nearby. Then I saw Mrs. A—she had the fishing pole in a death grip and was struggling with a big fish she had hooked. "I got him, I got him!" she yelled in delight as I ran down the dock towards her. "Get a net!" she shouted when she saw me.

Turning on my heel, I sprinted down the shore until I reached our dock, grabbed a net out of my dad's boat, and in a matter of moments I was back by Mrs. A's side. I stuck the net in the water at the end of the line and pulled up the biggest muskie I had ever seen. It took all my strength to hoist it onto the dock. "I finally got you, you old rascal!" she said, wagging her finger at the fish as I struggled to keep it under control.

Mrs. A's shouting and the racket we made landing the fish attracted the attention of my parents and a neighbor who was a part-time photographer for the local paper. They too had come to the dock to see what all the excitement was. As the photographer ran to get his camera, Mrs. A explained, "He's been swimming by my dock for years, teasing me, taunting me by splashing at the end of my dock and mocking my attempts to catch him. But no more, you rascal!!" she said, turning her attention to the fish once more. About this time the photographer returned and told me to hold up the fish, which I struggled but managed to do long enough to get a good photo that was published in the paper the next day.

When I asked Mrs. A if she intended to mount it she looked at me as if I had just asked her to pull her molars out. "My goodness, no! Back in the lake with him!"

I countered with, "But he could be a state record!"

"Nonsense!" she replied. Mrs. A didn't care about such things. We did manage to measure the fish before we released it and it was almost five feet long. Dad helped me get it back into the lake and he held its tail, which is what you do with such a large fish when it's been out of water too long. You do this until the fish is able to shimmy out of your hand and swim off on its own. Which after a minute he did, disappearing into the depths, but returning a minute later, leaping out of the water just yards off the end of the dock. After that, when Mrs. A read on her dock, she no longer had the pole.

A short time after the photograph of her and the muskie was taken, she suffered a bad fall and was laid up. I went to check on her everyday, helped her with what I could around the house, and would ride my bike into Eagle River and pick up some groceries for her. I was the only one she would allow to help her. After several weeks of this, Mrs. A got stronger and worked her way back to where she could walk and function normally again with only a cane for assistance. She asked me to run to town one last time, which I gladly did, and when I returned she invited me into her house and asked me to take a seat in the living room. She left the room for a moment and returned with a shoe box. "I am getting old," she began to explain, "and one day I will be gone, and people seem to be interested in my past. I've decided to leave my secret with you, but you cannot tell anyone until after I am gone. Not that they will believe you," she said with a mischievous smile. A cold shiver went down my spine. *What dark secret had this woman been guarding all these years?* I thought to myself.

Mrs. A opened the shoe box and right on top was an old black and white picture of three young ladies, all wearing flowing white dresses with their hair all made up. "This was taken in January 1917," she explained in her thick accent while showing me the photo. "I am the one sitting on the floor in the middle; the ones sitting in the chairs on either side of me are my sisters. This picture was taken at a ball in honor of my father at the royal palace at Mogilev. I am from Russia, and in the early 1900s my family was royalty. I was considered a princess."

Mrs. A paused for a moment to let this information sink in. I didn't know what to think. After several moments she continued. "It was here at this ball that I met the love of my life. I was only seventeen years old and I can remember clearly standing in the corner of the great ballroom. It was lit with gas lamps along the walls and had floor-to-ceiling windows where the light from the ballroom spilled out onto the fresh snow. It was a clear, cold night and a million stars were in the sky. I didn't think anything could be more perfect, when suddenly a tall, young man with dark hair and a beautiful smile came up to me and asked me to dance. His name was Rudi Alexiconofski, and he was from a well-to-do family from St. Petersburg. I was in love from the moment I first laid eyes on him. He came up to me and bowed like a perfect gentleman, then escorted me to the dance floor. As we waltzed I felt like the entire world had disappeared, and Rudi and I were the only ones left. The gas chandelier above us shone up onto the golden cherubs that hung above, and they looked down upon us as we moved across the beautiful hand-laid parquet floor. When it was over he bowed again and gently kissed my gloved hand. I was smitten. I was only seventeen but I knew right then and there I was going to marry Rudi.

"Father was against this, for in his eyes Rudi was not of noble birth. And his family was rumored to be involved with the Bolsheviks, who were circulating propaganda against my family. Before he left, Rudi and I made arrangements to meet. Back home in Moscow he would come by. I would put a candle in a window to signal where I was waiting for him. We were very sneaky. My cousin Maria would come over and sleep in my bed so it looked like I was there when mother would check on us. Rudi never failed to come. He always rode up on his white horse and off we would go riding through the streets of Moscow late at night.

"The world was collapsing around us, World War I was in its third year, and the Russian army was poorly supplied and not doing well against the Germans. Many soldiers had mutinied and fled their posts on the western front. There was talk of revolution, but none of it mattered to me; I was in love. In March of 1917 my father was forced to abdicate. Soon the Russian Revolution erupted and my father was arrested. We were taken to Yetakarinburg, and were kept under house arrest by the Bolsheviks in the home of a doctor. After several months and through the help of my cousin Maria I was able to contact Rudi and tell him where I was. I hoped and prayed he would come for me. I longed to see him. Day after day I would light a candle and place it in a window and watch for him. Months passed, finally an entire year, and I never got to see him.

"One night my cousin Maria showed up unexpectedly. She was dressed in dark clothes and she came to my bedroom window and tapped on it until I opened it. 'Get up and get dressed,' she whispered as she crawled in. I didn't ask what was happening and did as she said. She told me Rudi was waiting for me down the street in an alley. Anna put on my night gown and climbed into my bed to make it look like I was still there. I carefully snuck out past the guards and down the street where I found Rudi waiting. To my shock he was in the uniform of an army officer. Without a word he helped me up onto his horse then he got on behind me and we were off.

"After a few minutes we stopped at a small, dark house on the outskirts of town. We went in and I found myself in a brightly lit room with windows covered with sack cloth to keep the light from shining out onto the street. It was here Rudi asked me to marry him. I agreed without hesitation. We went into an adjoining room where the priest from the Orthodox church was waiting. Rudi's sister and brother were there too. They acted as the best man and maid of honor. Rudi gave me this ring," she said, showing me the ring on her finger. She also showed me a photo of her standing with a bouquet of flowers in her hand next to a tall, dark-haired, young man in a military-style uniform flanked by the maid of honor and the best man. Behind them stood a priest holding a tall pole with a Russian Orthodox crucifix on the top and dressed in dark clothes. Mrs. A and Rudi were smiling. Everyone else looked very serious.

Mrs. A continued, "After the ceremony, Rudi explained that he had joined the army and was fighting against the Bolsheviks and the revolution. Since he had been educated at the University of Moscow he was given an officer's commission. He told me he felt the fight against the revolutionaries was futile and that he and his family intended to escape out of Russia. He wanted me to come with him, and I agreed, but first I needed to go back and tell my parents. We got on his horse and rode back into Yetakarinburg. Arriving at the doctor's house, we discovered the armed guards were gone and the house was strangely dark. Rudi and I went in and searched the house. It was in disarray and everyone was gone. Then we went into the basement, where we found such horror. There was blood everywhere, on the floor and on the walls. Something unspeakable had happened. Rudi and I fled. We went back to the priest's house and Rudi put me in a carriage with his sister and brother. He instructed his brother to get me to safety. Before he left he told me he had a contingency of soldiers hiding nearby and he was going to take them and go looking for my family. He kissed my hand and told me not to worry, he would find me. Next he closed the carriage door and he was gone into the night.

"His sister, brother and I made it back to their family's home at St. Petersburg. That night we all left for the family cottage in Yuriatin on the other side of the Urals. I was inconsolable. My family was suddenly gone and it didn't look good. And now my Rudi was gone looking for them. It took us two weeks to get to the cottage at Yuriatin. The whole time I watched behind us to see if Rudi was following.

"We spent the next several months at the cottage, and it was during this time we received word that my parents, along with my sisters, brother and my cousin Maria, had been murdered. Poor Maria had been mistaken for me and suffered what would have been my fate. Apparently the Bolsheviks didn't know I wasn't there and just assumed Maria was me, because they were not looking for me. I also learned that Rudi had been captured and charged as a counter-revolutionary. As soon as we learned this, Rudi's father left Yuriatin and returned to St. Petersburg in an attempt to gain Rudi's freedom. He returned a month later. I knew as soon as I saw him that it was bad news. My darling Rudi had been executed. They wouldn't even let his father have his body for proper burial; the Bolsheviks threw my darling in a mass grave and buried him with other 'counter-revolutionaries' as an example. His father managed to see him before he was shot and he had given his father a single item and asked that he give it to me."

With that Mrs. A reached into the cardboard box and pulled out a small candle. "It told me that he would come for me," Mrs. A said. "I was so devastated, I didn't know what to do. My entire world was gone. What was worse was Rudi's dad told us that he had been ordered not to leave St. Petersburg, but he slipped out disguised as a refugee and made it back to us on the train. He felt that it was only a matter of time before they came for the rest of the Alexiconofski family. That very day he made arrangements and got me out of Russia, and with the help of some family friends, I was smuggled to Paris, where I was to wait for the family, but they never came. Years later I learned that they were all arrested the next day. I never heard from them again. No one knew who I was and I had used up all the money Rudi's father had given me. So I took a job and was able to support myself. After a few years I moved to England, and then I immigrated to the United States. I became a US citizen and worked a variety of jobs. During WWII I took a job at Boeing in Seattle and helped build the B-17 and B-29 bombers. After the war I stayed with Boeing and worked there for the next twenty years. Once, while in Wisconsin on vacation, I found this very house for sale. I bought it then and there and I have been here ever since. Your winters remind me of Russia."

I was at a loss. It was a bit overwhelming to think that a woman, who as long as I could remember had lived a simple life here on the shore of Pine Lake, who found great pleasure in simple things and whose independent nature only allowed her to ask for help of one young man when she was hurt, was once a member of the Russian royal family. My initial thought was to doubt, but the evidence was overwhelming; here were the pictures, here were the documents and here was the gentle old lady, whom I had known and trusted my whole life and who had risked her own life without hesitation to save mine, telling me it was true. It took me years to digest the magnitude of this secret, and until now I have never spoken of it.

There is one more page to this story, however. A year or two after Mrs. A revealed who she was to me, she died. I must admit I was heartbroken as I watched strangers come and close up her house and put it up for sale. Per her last will she was cremated, and to everyone's surprise but mine her ashes were taken to Russia and spread on a mass grave near St. Petersburg. At the time, Russia was still behind the "Iron Curtain" and there was a lot of red tape involved to get Mrs. A to her final resting place. But her attorney was insistent and finally achieved her last wishes. A week or so after Mrs. A was returned home to Russia, there was a knock on our door. I opened it up to find Mrs. A's attorney. He held the shoebox in his hand that Mrs. A had shown me as she told me her story. The attorney explained that the will stated that he was to give me the shoe box and that per Mrs. A, I "would know what to do with it." She was right.

That very evening I went out into a gentle snowstorm and through an old deer trail that connected our property to Mrs. A's. I took the candle out of shoe box, and using the hidden key, I let myself in. I placed the candle in the kitchen window that looked down the long driveway and lit it. I then left the house and was in the woods between our properties when suddenly I heard the unmistakable sound of a horse coming up her driveway. I watched in disbelief as a young man in a WWI Russian army uniform, complete with ceremonial saber, rode into view on a white horse. He rode up to the back of the house. At the same time I saw a very young Mrs. A, looking the same age she was in her wedding photo, come out of the house in the long white dress she had on at the ball so many years before. In her hand she held the candle I had just lit. The soldier got off the horse and lifted Mrs. A into the saddle then climbed on behind her. The soldier, who was undoubtedly her beloved Rudi, tipped his hat to me and then Mrs. A looked right at me and smiled. She blew out the candle and dropped it into the newly fallen snow. An instant later they were gone.

The house sold to another couple with a last name that started with "A," so they left the large letter on the house. They lived there for a number of years until they decided to move on. I never spoke of this story until now because I think Mrs. A would have wanted it that way. Later on I framed that newspaper article of her and her trophy muskie, and today it hangs in my office. When people ask me the story behind it I shrug and say with a smile, "Why that's Mrs. A and her trophy muskie."

The Night of the Panther

There once was a great showman who plied his trade along the many towns and villages that nestle along the shores of the Great Lakes. He traveled mostly by schooner or tramp steamer, and every summer he would take his show of exotic animals on tour. "Mighty James Dudeck," he called himself. "The Greatest Animal Trainer in the World" was his billing. He was a huge, good-natured man, with hands as big as early baseball mitts, a deep, hearty laugh and a smile to match. He loved to bring his animals on tour and charged people a very nominal fee to see them. He knew that people enjoyed seeing his lions and tigers and assorted smaller creatures, but the crowd pleaser was always his black panther. James Dudeck never felt it necessary to make large profits off of the many poor people that came to see his show. "Just enough to keep the show going," was what he would say. Children, especially, were his favorite. One time, a group of five young ones did not have enough money between them to attend. Dudeck made a huge display about how they couldn't come in if they didn't pay and, at the same time, he held open the flap to the big top and he himself ushered them to seats in the front row.

Dudeck indeed was well liked by all who came in contact with him. For nearly a decade during the late 1800s he and his wild animal show were a staple of summertime life along the Great Lakes.

One year Dudeck took his show to Isle Royale. Isle Royale, as you know, is an island in the northwest corner of Lake Superior, large enough to support inhabitants year-round. Here James

Dudeck met Frank Walker. Frank Walker was everything James Dudeck was not. Walker was a devious, sinful man driven by profit and self-promotion. He didn't care what he had to do or whom he had to step on to advance himself politically or financially. By the time these men met, Walker had already gotten himself appointed (through less than legal dealings) constable of the small Isle Royale settlement. Walker was familiar with Dudeck and thought him a fool for not charging people more to see his wild animals. Dudeck knew enough not to trust Walker.

As soon as Dudeck set up his big-top tent on Isle Royale, trouble began. The sheriff of the settlement, who just happened to be Walker's equally scheming brother-in-law, performed an inspection of Dudeck's tent and his animals. He issued citations for numerous violations, from littering to not paying taxes for use of public land and harboring dangerous animals. Dudeck was ordered to pay fines amounting to hundreds of dollars for these weak and trumped-up charges. Dudeck refused to pay, and after only one show, he packed up and loaded his animals onto the only passage he could find off the island: an old lumber schooner that had brought a load of wood to Isle Royale a few days earlier. Before Dudeck and his animals could leave, the sheriff arrested him and threw him in jail for refusing to pay his fines. Much to no one's surprise, it soon turned out that Walker himself was behind the sheriff's actions. Dudeck sat in the jail cell while Walker stood at the door puffing on a huge cigar and blowing big clouds of smoke into Dudeck's face.

"Why don't you sell me that show of yours?" Walker would ask with a wicked gleam in his eye. Dudeck refused to even answer. After several hours of this, Walker became bored with his harassment and told the sheriff to release Dudeck if he paid his fines. Dudeck, having no other alternatives, paid the blackmail and quickly left for the dock where the lumber schooner containing his animals was moored. The sun had already set by the time they set sail. They were out of the port no more than an hour when they ran into a heavy fog bank. The captain soon lost his way, and the schooner strayed into the main shipping lanes. The crew heard the freighter long before they could see it.

The captain furiously sounded the foghorn, but it was too late. Through the dense fog the crew watched in horror as the big steel bow of newer freighter emerged and stuck them amidships. The lumber schooner was deeply wounded and almost immediately went into her death throes. Dudeck, thrown to the deck by the impact, was badly injured, but still managed to crawl to the cages on deck and was able to open several before the ship made her final plunge. But it was all to no avail. The people on Isle Royale could not see but could clearly hear the agonizing cries of the animals as one by one they were sucked down along with the passengers and crew of the lumber schooner. The crew of the freighter tried in vain to locate survivors, but the thick fog prevented any chance of a rescue. She stood by until dawn came and burned off the fog. Morning found the freighter *Kamloops* surrounded by wreckage of the schooner, but no survivors. The surfboat rescue crew from Isle Royale came out and the only living thing they found was Dudeck's soaking-wet rabbit adrift on a broken piece of the ship's mast. They took the pathetic creature back to Isle Royale, where it was adopted by the daughter of the captain of the surfboat crew. She named it after the schooner and nursed it back to health.

Over the next several days, wreckage from the schooner washed ashore on Isle Royale. The residents of the Isle picked through the flotsam and salvaged what they could. Walker, the man that was directly responsible for the chain of events that led to sinking of the schooner, was walking along the beach with the sheriff, looking at the wreckage. Smoking on his big cigar, he said with an evil grin, "Bet that fool wishes he had sold me his show now." Suddenly Walker was startled by a figure dressed in ragged clothing standing in his path. It was the old beachcomber woman, Mattie. Mattie lived in seclusion on the north end of Isle Royale; she was rarely seen and thought to be more a legend than an actual person. People who had come in contact with her usually referred to her as "that old witch woman" because it was thought she practiced witchcraft.

In Mattie's hands was the ship's broken name board. Walker, too stunned by her sudden appearance, was speechless.

Mattie stared directly at Walker. "There has been a great injustice," she said in a raspy voice. "Lake Superior only takes the lives of those who don't respect her." She then slowly raised her arm and pointed a crooked, boney finger at Walker. "It was not Dudeck's fate to die in her frigid depths. She'll be coming for you, Walker." With that, Mattie hurled the board at Walker's feet and shuffled away. Walker managed to force out a weak, arrogant laugh as Mattie slipped into the forest.

A year to the day after the sinking, a terrific Nor'easter ravaged the island with vicious waves and torrential winds and rain for twenty-four hours straight. The next morning the sheriff was summoned by a local fisherman who lived just off the beach, where most of the wreckage of the lumber schooner washed ashore the previous year. The sheriff arrived to find the fisherman deeply agitated.

"What seems to be the problem?" the sheriff asked.

"Last night during that storm," he explained, "I heard terrific yowl of a wild animal like I never heard before."

The sheriff paused for a second, then asked in disgust, "You called me out here for that?"

"That ain't all," the fisherman retorted. With that, he headed off toward the beach. The sheriff followed. After walking about 100 feet to the edge of the water, the fisherman stopped and looked down. The sheriff looked down too and was amazed to see the largest set of paw prints he had ever seen. They led directly from the water, across the sandy beach, and up into the forest. On either side of the tracks were clumps of seaweed that looked as if it had dropped off the creature as it moved across the sand.

"How could these prints be here?" the sheriff asked. "That storm last night would have washed away everything."

The fisherman nodded his head. "Watch," was all he said. Just then a good-sized wave rolled ashore and covered the footprints. When it receded back into the lake the prints remained. The wave erased nothing. The footprints were completely unaffected.

The sheriff was obviously rattled by the strange prints, but tried to hide his fear. "You're makin' all this up," he said in an abusive tone.

"I guess I won't tell about the glowing red eyes then," was all the fisherman said as he walked away and left the sheriff on the beach. The sheriff quickly left and headed back to the settlement. Along the way numerous people stopped him and told about hearing strange animal noises during the night. One man reported hearing the sounds of a terrible fight in the woods that surrounded his cabin. In the morning, when he went to look, he found four dead timber wolves, all ripped to shreds. As the sheriff got closer to town he could not help but realize that whatever had come out of the lake was heading straight towards the settlement.

The sheriff reached his office to find Walker pacing nervously and puffing on his cigar. When he saw the sheriff he demanded, "What is going on? People have been coming up to me all morning with crazy stories about a huge, dark beast with glowing red eyes."

The sheriff nodded. "I heard the same stories. I'll get the best hunters on the island and we will go out looking for it." They started towards the door and were both taken aback to see Mattie, the old beachcomber, standing in the doorway, blocking their way out. "No need to go looking," she said in her raspy voice. "It intends to find you."

Walker found his voice. "Out of the way, you old hag," he demanded.

"I saw it last night," she continued. "It came right past my shack. A big black panther with glowing red eyes. There is no escape for you, Walker. Your time is at hand!"

"Go back to your side of the island, witch!" Walker shouted as he pushed his way past her.

Once outside, the sheriff approached several hunters and requested they join him on a search. Every single one of them refused. "Only a fool would hunt for such a creature," one man said. Finally the sheriff went into a small tavern and forced a hunter to help him. The man didn't want to go but he had a drinking problem and had been locked up by the sheriff several times and owed quite a bit of money in fines. The sheriff told him his debt would be forgiven if he helped. Reluctantly the man agreed. They left the settlement on foot, each carrying a high-powered rifle.

Several hours later the town folk could hear gunshots and the sound of a man screaming. No one was willing to go investigate. About an hour after, that tracker came back, alone and without his gun. He was severely distraught; he walked right past the crowd of people that had gathered and straight into the tavern. He ordered a drink, but his hand was shaking so much he got very little of it when he tried to down it. The crowd had followed him in to the bar, and finally someone asked, "What happened?"

The man managed to swallow the last few drops of the alcohol that remained in his glass, then turned and faced the crowd. "It was tracking us," he said. "It was on us as soon as we left the settlement. You could hear it circling us in the woods. It crept around us for hours as we hiked through the trees. Finally we came to a clearing, so we decided to try and ambush it. We waited and could hear it approaching. I saw it first, a big black panther with burning red eyes. I fired as it charged, I'm sure I hit it, but it was not affected. It ran right past me and knocked me down. It didn't want me." The man paused and signaled the bartender for another drink.

"Where is the sheriff?" someone asked.

The tracker took the shot of whiskey the barkeep had poured for him and downed it. "Dead, I hope," he replied. "That panther leaped and landed right on the sheriff. You could hear the sheriff's bones crunching as the animal chomped down on his thigh. He screamed as the panther drug him off. I couldn't keep up with them." The crowd gasped collectively and a murmur of voices filled the room as everyone started whispering at once. The tracker finished off a third shot of whiskey and slammed the glass down on the bar, bringing the room to sudden silence.

"There is something else," he said. "After I lost the trail of the panther and the sheriff, I thought I heard the sheriff scream one last time. Way off in the distance. He said something like, 'Walker, Walker, it's coming for you!'"

His words sent a chill through the room. Especially through Frank Walker, who was standing in the back of the room. He had followed the crowd into the tavern, and no one had noticed him until now. The crowd turned and looked at Walker. He said nothing. "You brought this scourge upon us," someone said.

"Nonsense," Walker replied. He turned and walked out of the tavern. The crowd followed. Walker reached the middle of the street, when suddenly he stopped. Something had caught his attention. It was now dusk and a low fog bank was creeping into the town. It moved quickly, and within minutes it had enveloped the entire settlement. Walker stood alone in the middle of the street. The crowd of people watched from the boardwalk as the fog covered the area from the ground to about four feet high. It was a thick, heavy fog and had an unusual greenish glow to it. Walker tried to walk back to his office but found he couldn't move. He was frozen in fear.

Suddenly everyone noticed something moving through the mist. You could hear whatever it was but you could not see it because it was low to the ground and concealed by the unearthly fog. People knew it was the panther. They strained to try and see it but the thickness of the fog prevented them from seeing even a glimpse. Soon it became apparent that it was circling Walker, as he stood there frozen like a statue. He could only hear it, just like the helpless men on the doomed lumber schooner could hear the steel freighter approach them. Walker was now equally helpless and he knew it. The townsfolk watched as suddenly the creature in the fog let go a low growl. They could see Walker look down, his eyes as wide as saucers, sheer terror written on his face. He started to shout something, but was quickly cut off as suddenly he was ripped from his feet and down into the fog. There were sounds of a tremendous scuffle, and people could hear Walker screaming and pleading as he was dragged off. No one dared follow.

The next morning all the men gathered with their guns and followed the creature's tracks. You could clearly see how Walker had been dragged out of the settlement. They expected to find his body somewhere in the forest. Much to everyone's surprise they didn't. They trail left by the animal led for miles, all the way to the shore of Lake Superior. Here they could clearly see where Walker had been dragged into the water. Nearby lay the only thing of Walker's ever found, his cigar.

The men stood there at the water's edge and talked among themselves, trying to fathom this strange course of events, when Mattie was seen approaching. She reached the group, and without a word of greeting, said, "You're safe now. Superior has claimed her debt." With that, she turned around and headed back towards her side of the island.

Years passed and the panther was never seen or heard from again. The bodies of Frank Walker and his brother-in-law sheriff were never found. However, during the 1980s, wreck divers discovered the remains of the ill-fated lumber schooner. She lay in about seventy-five feet of water, and several animal cages were found in the wreckage. One cage in particular still carried the sign

"Panther," and after almost 100 years on the bottom of the lake, it could clearly be seen that the cage was still locked. Surprisingly, inside the cage were not the bones of any animal. Instead there were two human skeletons. The mouths of both skulls were open in a screaming gesture, frozen in undeniable expressions of intense fear and agony. Lake Superior had indeed claimed her debt.

The Mysterious Flyer

Summer had come to the shores of Catfish Lake, and since the last of the snow had now disappeared and the lightning bugs had laid claim to Vilas County, our five adventurers, Maggie, Doug, Sarah, Charlie and Billy, had packed away their snowmobiles and their winter gear and gotten out their bicycles. It was a warm day, and they decided to ride their bikes into town and do what kids do, which is, of course, "hang out." They were all fooling around in small park along the Wisconsin River that was once the location of Duffy's Tavern, when they suddenly noticed an old woman standing on the bridge, dropping flowers one by one into the river. She was surrounded by what appeared to be her family, and they were all holding a single flower, which they threw in when the old lady was done dropping hers in.

"What's up with that?" asked Maggie.

Nobody answered her; they just all watched the strange ceremony as it unfolded. Before the flowers even floated by the park, the kids were back to playing.

Later on that evening, back at their homes on the shore of Catfish Lake as they sat around the fire pit, Billy suddenly spoke up.

"I had this weird dream last night," he said to no one in particular. "I dreamed I was sleeping and that I woke up and looked out the window and there was some guy standing out in the yard. He motioned for me to follow him, and as I watched, he walked down to the lake and then he walked out across the water and headed off in the direction of the far side."

"You mean he swam across the lake?" Charlie asked.

"No," Billy replied, "he walked on the water."

"I've had that same dream," Maggie said. "Just a couple of nights ago. It seemed so real."

Just then the kids heard Maggie and Sarah's parents talking in the kitchen.

"It was the weirdest thing," they heard the mother say. "I had this dream that there was this man standing in the yard and he looked right at me then he walked out across the lake."

The kids all stared at each other; this was way too much of a coincidence to ignore. So they formulated a plan: after their parents went to bed they were going to sneak out and watch for this mysterious figure.

"Who do you think he is?" Billy asked.

"Was," Sarah said. "I bet he is a ghost."

"Ohh . . ." Billy lamented. "Why can't we go looking for something not so scary? . . . Like a grizzly bear or a rabid mountain lion.

At around eleven o'clock, with remarkable stealth, all the kids managed to sneak out of their houses without their parents hearing and met near an old boat that was sitting in Maggie and Sarah's yard.

"What do we do now?" Doug asked.

"Hide and watch," Maggie replied.

They only had to wait a few minutes, when suddenly they heard the sound of something moving towards them from the direction of the lake.

"SSSHHHHHH!" Sarah whispered. "It's coming"

The kids peered over the boat into the darkness. They strained to see in the moonless night.

Whatever it was, it got closer and closer, and the kids got more and more anxious. Suddenly, Doug could not stand the tension any longer. He snapped on a flashlight he had brought along. It revealed a large, furry, dark creature.

"BEAR!!" they all said in unison.

Before they had a chance to react, the bear, equally as startled as the kids were, turned tail and ran away back into the darkness. The kids started to laugh at their close call when suddenly Doug felt someone grab his arm. It was Charlie—he was grabbing Doug's arm and was trying to speak, but all he could do was make unintelligible sounds. Doug turned around and instantly saw why Charlie was trying to get his attention. Standing behind them, not six feet away, was the glowing figure of a man. Doug, equally as speechless as Charlie, grabbed Maggie's arm, and so on until all the kids were facing the apparition. The ghost looked squarely at them then slowly raised its arm as if to point at something. Billy was the first to find his voice. "Run!" he said as he bolted for home. The kids all scattered and ran home. Amazingly, they all got back inside without waking up their parents.

The next day the boys left their home and walked the short path through the woods to Maggie and Sarah's house. Maggie and Sarah were already outside waiting for them.

They compared notes to what they had seen the night before. Most everyone was too scared to notice anything unusual, but Charlie said, "He was wearing a flight suit. I got a good look at him."

"A flight suit?" Sarah asked.

"Yeah," Charlie replied. "Like the kind you see people wearing in those old WWII movies."

"I think we need to go to the library," Maggie said.

After breakfast they all rode into Eagle River to the town library. After a couple hours of searching and a little help from Matilda the librarian, they found a newspaper article from 1944. It stated that a Navy fighter pilot had flown his aircraft to St. Germain to visit his wife and new baby. He was supposed to fly from the St. Germain Airport to Eagle River Airport to refuel but never made it. The Wisconsin River was over flood stage at that time and it is believed he crashed into the river and was swept away. This theory is based on some damaged tree tops found along the river. They think his plane clipped the trees and went in.

"That lady at the bridge yesterday," Billy said. "The one throwing flowers in the river. I bet that was his wife, and the rest of the people must be his family."

Everybody nodded in agreement.

"So you think his plane is in Catfish Lake?" Doug asked.

"Couldn't be," replied Maggie. "Catfish is only about twenty feet deep at its deepest point. Someone would have seen it in the last sixty years. Besides, the damaged trees were along the river, and Catfish Lake is miles from there."

After returning from the library, Doug asked Billy, "Where did that guy walk to?"

"Straight across," Billy replied.

Maggie went in her house and came back with a map of the lake. Spreading it out on the picnic table, she asked Billy, "Which direction did your ghost head?"

Billy indicated a direction and five sets of eyes traced an imaginary line from the docks near their homes to the direction he indicated.

"The swamp," they all said in unison. On the far side of the lake was a marshy area that no one ever went into.

Without a word, they all headed to the dock, and in a few moments were rowing their way across the lake.

They reached the edge of the swamp and tied the boat off to a tree. Charlie, being the lightest, was the first to set foot on the spongy ground.

"Stay spread out," he said.

The swamp was surrounded by a ridge that was solid in some areas but soft and mushy in others. The kids cautiously worked their way around the ridge as far as they thought safely possible. After a several hours of searching they found nothing that would indicate an aircraft or anything else had ever been there. The sun had just started to set, and they got in the boat to leave when Maggie suddenly jumped out of the boat.

"He's here," she shouted, almost in disbelief.

Everyone scrambled out of the boat, and to their surprise, they saw the ghostly image of the pilot standing on the ridge, beckoning them to follow. He led the kids to an area heavily overgrown by trees and vines; it is here the pilot simply vanished. In the fading light they pushed their way into the heavy undergrowth.

"I see it!" Billy and Maggie shouted together. There, half buried in the swamp, covered in vines and other overgrowth, was the lost fighter plane. For sixty years it had lain where it crashed, undisturbed, waiting in silence for someone to come find it.

The next day a media circus descended upon Catfish Lake. Camera crews from all over Wisconsin and Michigan came to cover the story. When asked how they found the plane, Maggie, acting as the spokesman, told them, "We were just exploring along the swamp and saw it."

Later on Sarah asked, "Why did you not tell them about the ghost?"

"We don't need the kind of attention that would bring to Catfish," she explained. "Besides, I think we've seen the last of our ghost."

A few days later the Navy came and removed the pilot and took him to St. Germain to be buried with full military honors. Our five adventurers were the guests of honor and earned the eternal gratitude of the pilot's family. Later on the Navy recovered the fighter plane and took it to a museum in Pensacola, Florida.

About a week after all the excitement settled down, Doug,

Charlie and Billy made their way down the path that led to a dock that their two homes on the lake shared. It was early evening, about the same time of day that they had found the missing plane weeks before. To their surprise, Maggie and Sarah were already there. Without a word they all walked out to the end of the big dock and looked to the southwest, as if expecting something to happen. And happen it did; a moment later a WWII fighter roared into sight right over the trees, skimmed over the lake at about 300 miles per hour and pulled up just as it got to the dock, "buzzing" the kids. They turned around just in time to see it disappear over the trees.

Charlie nodded his head. "I knew he would come say thanks."

Everyone nodded in agreement.

As Maggie had predicted, they never saw the ghostly figure of the pilot again. The old woman at the bridge died a short time later and was buried alongside her long-lost pilot husband. The plane, recovered from the swamp, was restored and now sits proudly in the Naval Air Museum in Florida, the name of the pilot, missing for so long, painted beneath the cockpit. As for our five adventurers, they were glad when the tranquility returned to Catfish Lake. But as everyone knows, it won't be long before another adventure will present itself. Hopefully, it won't be that rabid mountain lion . . .

Fall Comes to Vilas

Let me start this story by saying my family is lucky. Not that we are rich or famous or anything—we are lucky because my two brothers, sister and I were born to parents who were loving and caring and had foresight.

Dad had worked for the railroad, not on a train but as a salesman that traveled the Midwest selling space on boxcars to businesses who sought to move their products to market. Fresh from four years in the Navy, he would have rather been an engineer, I am sure, but the railroad wasn't offering that job, so he took the sales job. On one of his very first trips around the state calling on clients he happened into a small diner outside of Eagle River, Wisconsin, and it was here he met Mom working the counter. Dad walked in, their eyes met and it was love at first sight.

After one "textbook" whirlwind romance they moved into a small house in southeastern Wisconsin and started a family. Four kids and two basset hounds later, Dad noticed that Mom seemed to long for her home in Vilas County, so, leaving us in the care of an aunt, they traveled to Vilas and found a tired cottage on a small lake of about 110 acres, east of Eagle River. This is what is referred to as a three-season home, meaning you're nuts if you try to stay in it during the winter months. So this became our vacation home.

Dad's income was stretched thin raising us so there was not a lot of money to be spent on fancy amenities, and as a result the cottage only got what was required to keep it safe and habitable. Mom could not have been happier even if it were a castle. Even though we did not live there year round it was enough to get her back to the place she knew and loved, and in just the right dosage.

Dad created a ritual that we performed at the beginning of every summer; he told us there was a "lake spirit" and that in order to have good fishing we had to present a gift to this spirit. The gift was a small canoe paddle that we had to decorate in some fashion. Some years we painted scenes of sunsets and fish and birds on it; another time we used a wood burner to score images into the wood. We would then get a good fire going in the fire pit and draw straws. The winner got to put the paddle into the fire, thus making the sacrifice.

Another ritual that Dad created was in order to prove yourself worthy to fish on the lake, you had to hike through what Mom called "spirit woods." This was about a five-acre wooded area that bordered our property, surrounded on three sides by roads and one by the lake. If you could hike across these woods alone you were pronounced "worthy." It was all in good fun and we kids just ate it up.

Well, the sad thing about time is that it does not stop or even slow down for anyone. We all grew up. My two brothers moved out of state, our parents retired to Florida and my sister became custodian of the cottage. She, of course, kept the welcome mat out for everyone. She married and had two daughters, I married and had three boys, and today we take our kids to the lake as often as we can. Usually we share about a week together at the property in early summer and another one in fall.

During fall, I always find myself in reflection of the lazy days of summer we had spent on these grounds. Days filled with endless hours boating, campfires, ghost stories, hikes in the woods and of course fishing. As summer passed it became harder and harder to ignore the fact that the long shadows of evening appeared a little bit earlier every day, announcing the sun's departure from the skies over the North Woods. It was undeniable; fall was approaching.

Most welcomed the season with its cooler temperatures and its dazzling displays of foliage. But for as long as I could remember, fall was the season I dreaded.

Now I don't think everything about fall is bad and after the initial change of gears things go back into a routine that one quickly adjusts to. Well, until winter sets in, that is. One fall evening I found myself engaged in my favorite pastime, exploring the many trails that wound through the woods near our vacation home with my metal detector. I had done this dozens of times over the years and never failed to find something new or interesting. Today's discoveries were no different: a few old coins, a handful of bullets dropped by a hunter many decades before and a copper arrowhead lost by a Native American hunter centuries before. I considered these all good finds but even this could not help me shake the blue feeling I was having that summer had come to a close.

The sun was setting and I could feel the temperature starting to drop, and it was clearly time to make my way to the cottage. I took the trail that paralleled the shore so I could watch the sun set, and it was along this trail that to my surprise I spotted just up from the shore what appeared to be an actual Indian dwelling constructed so its opening faced the lake. There was a thin trail of smoke rising from that side. I figured it was just some kids from one of the cabins down the shore but my curiosity was piqued and I just had to take a look. Leaving the trail and quietly approaching the lodge, I heard a voice suddenly call out to me, "Come join me, friend."

Stepping around to the lake side, I saw an older gentleman sitting cross legged in front of a small fire. He wore buckskin, and a bear hide was draped across his shoulder. A single feather of black and white hung from his braided hair and rested near the front of his shoulder. In his left hand he held the bowl of a clay pipe with the other end clamped in his mouth. He nodded to a spot near the fire, indicating a place for me to sit. He took one last pull on his pipe, set it down on a nearby rock and started to speak.

"I am called Jacques, and this is my lake."

I could not help but notice he clearly was not French, nor had I ever seen him before so I was certain it wasn't "his" lake. He must have anticipated what I was thinking because he continued with, "My father was a French explorer and my mother was an Ojibwa. Growing up I was considered an outcast by the other children in our village, so I spent a lot of time exploring the woods and hunting. One day I was stalking the biggest buck I had ever seen. He stayed just out of reach and every time I thought I had a good shot at him he moved. Eventually I followed him all the way to the shore of this very lake and then he quickly vanished into the forest. Since it was not connected to any other lake, no one had ever seen it before. So this is where I came to get away from those that despised me. When I was old enough, I laid claim to the lake."

I nodded in understanding, not certain where he was going with all this nonsense. He continued. "It was here I built this lodge and married a girl whose father was also a Frenchman; she too was driven out from our village and found this lake while following the very same deer. We live in harmony with the lake and raised our children here. My father was a woodsman and taught me the skills I needed to provide for my family even in the leanest of winters. Every evening my wife and I would sit just as we are now and watch the sun set over our lake. The deer would always come to feed nearby and sometimes even a bear would come down to the lake to drink. We were happy here and dwelled on the shore of this lake for many, many years."

It was at this moment I heard the distinct call of the loon, and to my surprise it came from very close to where I was sitting. Peering in the fading light I could see the bird just yards from shore. "I think it's looking for its mate," I said.

The old Indian just nodded his head. "He will be along soon," he replied. Then changing the subject he looked at me and asked, "Why do you not like fall?"

The question caught me off guard, and instead of answering him, I asked, "How do you know I don't care for fall?"

He just nodded and with just the trace of a smile, he replied, "I can tell. It's in the way you look at the lake, it's in the way you walk in the forest. It tells me your heart is full of sorrow at the changing of the season. And you worry about what the future will hold."

I nodded my head but didn't say anything. He was more right than even I realized. He continued, "I have seen more years pass at this lake than I can even remember. I welcome the change if for no other reason than it makes one appreciate the seasons and their individual beauty. But I ask you this: If you are tired, do you not sleep?"

I nodded.

"This lake is no different, for it, too, is a living thing that sleeps under a blanket of ice and snow. And in spring when the ice breaks up the lake will be born anew. The deer and the bear will return to drink from the lake and play along the shore, and the fish will once again dance upon the water. It has never failed and it never will. And one more thing: Is it better to have known this lake and be here to witness the changing of the seasons even though they can bring some sadness, or is it better to not have ever known this lake?"

At this point the loon called out again, this time much louder and closer. "I have one last thing I must show you," he said. He stood up and reached for the flap of cloth that partially covered the opening to his dwelling and motioned for me to look inside. I ducked through the opening. In a moment my eyes adjusted and I could see the numerous decorated paddles hanging on the walls.

"Hey!" I exclaimed with a mixture of surprise and excitement as I recognized them, for these were the very same paddles that my siblings and I had "sacrificed" to the lake spirit decades before. I turned to look at the old Indian but he was gone, and a branch from

136

a nearby tree was holding the flap of the lodge open. I stepped back into the dimming light of evening. "Where did you go?" I called out.

A quick search around the lodge and the camp turned up nothing; he had simply disappeared. Suddenly the loon called out again, but this time the mate answered, and a second later it swooped in from just above the trees where I was standing. I happened to look down at that moment and at my feet lay the black and white feather the Indian had been wearing. As I picked it up I realized it was a loon feather. A moment later the two birds called out together, and as the last of the sun's rays faded, I saw them take flight and land on the far side of the lake. I suspect in a day or two they made their way to warmer climates to wait out the cold.

It was then that the changing of the seasons didn't seem so sad to me anymore. Perhaps the words of the old Indian made sense, for isn't change better than stagnation? I turned away from the lake and noticed the lodge, too, had vanished. In fact, all that remained was the Indian's old clay pipe, still sitting on the rock he had laid it on. I left it there, for the owner would be back to claim it in spring when the lake would break free of winter's icy grip and be born anew. And I knew I would return as well, as would my boys and maybe someday their descendants, too. I am good with this thought.

Grabbing my metal detector I headed for the cottage mindful of two things I was now certain of: Lamenting the passing of time is wasted time, and my encounter with the "lake spirit" would stay my secret for at least a while.